RED

DIAPER

BABY

red diaper baby
the mathematics of change
haiku tunnel

mercury house
san francisco

Red Diaper Baby

3 *comic* monologues *by*

Josh Kornbluth

Published in the United States by
Mercury House, San Francisco, California,
a nonprofit publishing company devoted
to the free exchange of ideas and guided
by a dedication to literary values.

United States Constitution, First Amendment:
Congress shall make no law respecting an
establishment of religion, or prohibiting the
free exercise thereof; or abridging the freedom of
speech, or of the press; or the right of the people
peaceably to assemble, and to petition the
Government for a redress of grievances.

Designed by Thomas Christensen in Adobe Futura.

LIBRARY OF CONGRESS CATALOGING-IN-PUBLICATION DATA:
Kornbluth, Josh.
Red Diaper Baby : three comic monologues /
by Josh Kornbluth. — 1st ed.
p.   cm.
Contents: Red diaper baby—The
mathematics of change—Haiku tunnel.
ISBN 1-56279-087-0 (pbk. : alk. paper)
1. Autobiography—Drama.
2. Autobiography—Humor.
3. Monologues.
I. Title.
PS3561.O675R43   1996
812'.54—dcB
[20]   96-23016
CIP

FIRST EDITION
9 8 7 6 5 4 3 2 1

for
SARA

Contents

red diaper

baby

My father, Paul Kornbluth, was a Communist.

He believed there was going to be a violent Communist revolution in this country—and that I was going to lead it. Just so you can get a sense of the pressure.

And anything my father told me I'd believe, because my father was such a physically magnificent man: he was big, and he had this great big potbelly—not a wiggly-jiggly, Social Democratic potbelly; a firm, Communist potbelly. You bopped it, it would bop you back. It was *strong.*

He had powerful legs, from running track at the City College of New York. And he had these beefy arms. And he was naked—virtually all the time; naked in the apartment. And all over his body he had these patches of talcum powder—you know, Johnson's Baby Powder—I guess because he was a big man and he would chafe. Especially around his private parts.

And he had me on the weekends. I would have loved to have slept in late on the weekends, but I couldn't because my father wouldn't let me. He would wake me up.

This is how he'd wake me up: he'd come bursting into my room and then he'd stop in the doorway; and when he stopped, the talcum powder would come bouncing off of his balls—it was like the entrance of a great magician. And then he'd come running up to my bed, and looming over me he'd sing:

> Arise, ye prisoner of starvation!
> Arise, ye wretched of the earth!

I didn't know that was the "Internationale"; I didn't know that was the international Communist anthem. I thought it was my own personal wake-up song.

Check it out: "Arise, ye prisoner of starvation"—it's time for breakfast. "Arise, ye wretched of the earth"—it's five o'clock in the morning and I'm being woken up!

And if I didn't show the proper signs of life right away, my father would lean down over me—and his long, graying hair would straggle down, his beard would flutter down into my nose—and he'd yell, "Wake up, Little Fucker! Wake up, Little Fucker!"

That was his nickname for me: Little Fucker. Nothing at all pejorative about it, as far as my father was concerned. For my dad, calling me "Little Fucker" was like calling me "Junior" . . . "Beloved Little One" . . . "Little Fucker."

I knew from an early age that one day I must grow up and become . . . a Big Fucker. And I assumed that that would be around the time that I would lead the Revolution. Because my dad had told me over and over that all the great revolutionaries were also great fuckers.

But for now I was just lying there in my bed, my father looming over me with his—to me—enormous penis . . . swinging around, spewing smoke, powder, whatever . . . while I just had this little, six-year-old . . . training penis, if you will.

"Little Fucker." I didn't realize at the time that my father had his own language—not only his own English, but his own Yiddish. I used to think it was real Yiddish, but then my mom would say, "That's not Yiddish. What your father speaks is not

Yiddish. *I* went to Yiddish school in Bensonhurst—and what your father speaks is not Yiddish."

I'd say, "You mean, *ouska* is not—"

"No. There's an *oyska*, but there's no *ouska*. . ."

Well, in my father's Yiddish, there was a term *ouska*. *Ouska* was a prefix, meaning "a lot of," "very"—as in, "I am ouska-cold, my son!"

I'd say, "Of course you're ouska-cold, Dad; you're ouska-naked. The window is ouska-open."

As it would be in the kitchen, where we'd go for breakfast. Dad and I would sit around the kitchen table having hard-boiled eggs (my father, not a soft-boiled kind of guy). And never little eggs: when Dad went shopping for eggs, he always got ouska-jumbo-large-size eggs, so we would not want for eggs. And we would smear on our eggs, in my father's language, "salad dress-ing"—meaning mayonnaise. And we'd drink juice—apple juice, orange juice . . .

And Dad would regale me with his stories of organizing in the South with the Henry Wallace campaign. (That's *Henry* Wallace. *Henry.* Okay?) And he'd drill me over and over in the catechisms of our faith—of Communism. Like how society has been driven from one stage to the next, driven inexorably by the forces of dialectical materialism, until . . .

I sense I'm covering old ground. But just to review:

According to Marx and Engels—and my dad—the first human society was Primitive Communalism: everyone's just kind of dancing around, like at a Grateful Dead concert.

The next stage after Primitive Communalism was Slavery—which must have been a bummer of a transition.

Then from Slavery to Feudalism, and from Feudalism ... Well, we've learned from history that it's very important after Feudalism to stop in Capitalism before moving on to Socialism. Very important to stop in Capitalism. Because that's where you get your appliances.

So you stop in Capitalism, you get your stuff, and *then* you move on to Socialism, and finally to Communism—and you're back at the concert.

After breakfast, me and my dad would move from the kitchen into the living room—although when I say "kitchen" and "living room," I'm being euphemistic. There was one basic room—except for my bedroom: Dad always insisted that I have my own bedroom for my privacy—he'd just come bursting in at any moment. But aside from my bedroom, there was just one basic room. That's because when my father moved into an apartment, the first thing he'd do is he'd knock down all the walls. I don't mean that metaphorically; he'd *knock down* all the walls.

The first time he did this, we had to move—right away. Because we lived on the first floor, and the building came . . . ouska-down.

So we moved into the next building—same landlord, who insisted on giving my dad a lecture on the crucial architectural concept of the supporting wall. That's the wall you must not knock down.

So my dad went knocking around with his hammer to find the

one wall that wasn't hollow, left that wall up, knocked down all the other walls. And all along the external walls of our kitchen-cum-bathroom-cum-living-room-cum-dining-room area were posters of our heroes, our gods: W. E. B. Du Bois, Malcolm X, Dr. King, Ho Chi Minh, Bertolt Brecht, Emma Goldman ... And then, at the end of all these posters: my height chart. See how the Little Fucker measures up.

And then we'd go outside for our walks. When we went outside, my father—in his one true concession to society—would put on clothing. This is back in '65, when I was about six years old. Dad wore this one-piece, bright orange jumpsuit—a parachute outfit—with a broad collar and a big zipper with a peace-symbol pull-thing that would seal in the freshness of the powder.

Being Communists, we had songs associated with every activity. But me and Dad didn't just have generic walking songs; we had specific going-up-the-hill songs, specific going-down-the-hill songs. We had learned our biggest going-up-the-hill song off an album by Paul Robeson, a great Jewish folksinger. It was a record my dad had borrowed from the public library, and then—as a revolutionary act—refused to return. (And my mom was a librarian ...)

Going up the hill, me and my dad would sing:

Ey yuch nyem
Ey yuch nyem
O Volga, Volga
Ey yuch nyem.

Very hard to walk fast while singing *"Ey Yuch Nyem."*

A lot easier on our going-down-the-hill song, which we had learned off an album by Doc Watson—a great Jewish folksinger from the Appalachians (another record that my dad had liberated from the library).

Going down the hill, me and my dad would sing:

> As I go down in the valley to pray
> Studying—

—as we went down in the valley to pray on East Seventh Street, between C and D—

> As I go down in the valley to pray
> Studying about that good old way
> And who shall wear the robe and crown
> Good Lord, show me the way.

My father couldn't hear me. He thought I wasn't singing. He didn't connect it with the fact that he was singing so ouska-loud he was drowning me out. So periodically he'd turn to me on the sidewalk and go, "Sing louder, my son—I can't hear you!"

> Oh, fathers, let's go down
> Let's go down, come on down.
> Oh, fathers, let's go down
> Down in the valley to pray.

"Try singing even louder, my son—and perhaps with more
. . . melodic invention."

So I'd go,

> Come on, fathers, let's go *down!*
> Down in the valley to pra-a-a-ay . . . to pray-yee!

"And a child shall lead them!" my dad would say, and then
we'd hit the flatlands of Manhattan, as we continued north on our
walks towards Herald Square. And along the flatlands we'd sing
what, for us, were "flat" songs—rounds—which were easier for
me, more even between the two singers. And along the flatlands
we would stop at the bodega to pick up supplies, and we'd stop
at the pharmacy to get Dad's pills—and we'd continue north
along the flatlands, singing rounds like:

> Come follow, follow, follow, follow, follow, follow me.
> Whither shall I follow, follow, follow
> Whither shall I follow, follow thee?
> To the greenwood, to the greenwood
> To the greenwood, greenwood tree!

A nice, cheerful walking song—though confusing lyrically, to
an urban child. "Follow thee to the greenwood tree"—why? I'd
much rather follow thee to, say, Chock Full O' Nuts.

Which was the kind of place we had to eat, me and Dad, because we had to live ouska-cheaply. Because my father . . .

Well, he was a schoolteacher—he was a very good school-teacher. But my dad would get a job and be teaching his students with great passion, but at the same time he would be developing this *anger* towards his bosses: the principal, the assistant principals, the school board. And this anger at his bosses would build and build, until finally Dad couldn't take it anymore. This would take about two weeks. And at the end of those two weeks, Dad would go storming into the principal's office and yell, "Fuck you!"

Often the guy would never have seen my dad before. And he'd say, "You're fired! . . . If you work for me, you're fired!"

And then Dad would get another job, and he'd be teaching his new students with great passion but developing this anger towards his *new* bosses. And at the end of two weeks he would storm into his new principal's office and go, "Fuck you!"

And the new principal would go, "You're fired!"

So Dad would find another job—perhaps a little farther away from New York, as he lost his license to teach in this gradually growing radius. And at the end of two weeks at his new job:

"Fuck you!"

"You're fired!"

And another job:

"Fuck you!"

"You're fired!"

And another:

"Fuck you!"

"You're fired!"

This went on for years and years; my father never saw . . . the pattern. He never saw the cause-and-effect between "Fuck you!" and "You're fired!"

So we had to live ouska-cheaply. Which was fine with me: I loved eating at places like Chock Full. You could have a nice hot dog, maybe some coconut cake . . . then we'd continue north for further ouska-cheap adventures, like the Museum of Natural History—where at the time the admission was whatever you would care to donate. They've since changed that policy—I think because of my dad. ("Pay them a penny and not a penny more, Fucker!" "You're right, Dad! We're not gonna give in to those imperialistic paleontologists!")

We'd go running up to the dinosaur exhibit, where Dad would give me a tour. I don't think he was an expert in the field, but he did have his bright orange tour-guide outfit. "The Tyrannosaurus rex, my son—one of the largest . . . reptilian fuckers ever to walk the earth!" And other little kids would break away from their field trips and join us. The field was a lot more interesting the way my dad described it.

And then, after a weekend of this kind of ouska-fun, my dad—as the courts had mandated—had to return me to . . . my mom.

My mom, Bernice "Bunny" Selden: also Jewish, also a New Yorker, also a City College grad, also a Communist—but so different from my father in temperament. If my father was an out-there, ouska Communist, my mom . . . *inska.*

And she had her own inska wake-up song for me, too—and like I thought Dad had written the "Internationale" for me, I thought my mom had written *her* wake-up song for me; I only found out years later that Irving Berlin wrote it.

My mom would be getting ready to go to work at the library across the river. She'd go into the bathroom in her nightgown and come back out with her hair in a bun. Then she'd go back into the bathroom and come out . . . with *another* bun having been added, from some mysterious source. And she'd stand in my open doorway—which was easy for her to do, because for some reason she would not let me have a door. And she'd tiptoe up to my bed and she'd lean down and sing:

> Oh, how I hate to get up in the morning
> Oh, how I'd love to stay in bed
> For the hardest blow of all
> Is to hear that bugler call:
> "You gotta get up, you gotta get up,
> You gotta get up in the morning."
>
> "You gotta get up, you gotta get up,
> You gotta get up in the morning."

A pretty nice wake-up song. Unless you know the second verse, which to me gets to a surreal level of violence that I find almost Sam Peckinpah-esque:

Someday I'm gonna murder the bugler
Someday you're gonna find him dead
I'll amputate his reveille
And stamp upon it heavily
And spend the rest of my life in bed!

I thought she could snap at any moment. So I'd get out of bed; I didn't want my reveille amputated!

But I still didn't have that get-up-and-go that the "Internationale" gives a kid. So she'd guide me gently up from my bed and lead me into the living room and sit me down on the couch, and then—this goes back to when I was at least four or five—she had this little motherly trick she'd play to get me going in the morning: she'd serve me a tall cup of double-espresso—with whipped cream and a maraschino cherry on top, because I'm a little kid!

And I'd sit there sipping my double-espresso on the couch, beneath the half-dozen or so ceramic disks that she bought in Mexico, where she went to divorce my dad—which, by the way, was when I was six months old.

They were married for nine years, then I was born—then, when I was six months old, they divorced. From time to time I'd wonder why.

But then, a few months ago, I was reading this article in the *Village Voice* about a guy named Saul Newton, a crazed psychoanalyst who ran this psychoanalytical cult called the Sullivanians. They had a co-op on the Upper West Side. I was reading about this Saul Newton guy, and how he told his patients that the family is evil—parents are intrinsically evil, and they can only wreak havoc on their children; you must break up the family.

Reading about this guy—Saul Newton, Saul Newton, Saul Newton—and suddenly it hit me: "Wait a second! My *dad's* therapist was named Saul!" So I called up my mom and said, "Mom, I'm reading about this Saul Newton guy," and she said, "Yeah, that was your father's therapist."

Evidently Dad was an early patient of Saul's—sort of a test case. And after I was born, Saul convinced my dad that now that he had a family, and families were evil, his family must be broken up. So Dad left me and my mom up in Washington Heights and he got an apartment down on the Lower East Side.

And then, according to my mom, after a couple of weeks Dad started to miss us. He came running up the island to try to reconcile with us. But Mom saw him coming and escaped with me down to Mexico, where she got the divorce, bought big floppy hats, danced around in circles with strangers, and got the half-dozen or so ceramic disks—each one of which depicts a woman escaping from slavery.

So I'd sit there under the disks on the couch, sipping my double-espresso, as my mom went up to the old radio console and turned on WBAI—listener-sponsored, sometimes listener-taken-over WBAI. The morning disc jockey at the time was Julius Lester—he of the ouska-deep voice. And supposedly, Julius's program was a classical-music show. But what Julius would do is, he'd play about five minutes of a Baroque oboe concerto . . .

and then speak for hours, about his various ex-wives and their sexual peccadilloes.

And I'd listen real carefully to Julius, and I'd sip my double-espresso, and I'd listen to Julius, and I'd sip my double-espresso . . . and then I'd go running off to school—jazzed!

I was so excited my first day of kindergarten. After spending the first five years of my life exclusively in the company of my parents and their friends, that day—for the first time—I was going to get to mingle with the masses.

Boy, was I disappointed! That first day, I walked into my kindergarten classroom at P.S. 128—and I saw all these little kids running around screaming, pulling hair, bopping each other, crying. I thought, "How will I ever organize *these* people?"

Fortunately, they had hired someone for that very purpose: Mrs. Spielhagen. She sat us down in a circle, and then—I guess, to get us centered that first day—she had us each say in turn what we wanted to be when we grew up. There was doctor, ballerina, fireman . . .

"Joshy?"

"A Big Fucker!"

Suspended! I think I'm still the only person in the history of New York State to be suspended on the first day of kindergarten. I was banished to the assistant principal's office, where I was assigned to fingerpaint moodily in isolation. (By the way, if there are any visual artists here, I think you'll back me up on this: it's very hard to do Socialist Realism in fingerpaints—very hard to get that nobility, that delineation . . .)

And I sat there, fingerpainting, thinking: "Why? Why am I being persecuted so? Just for saying what I'm going to physically be?"

That's all I thought I'd done: I mean, you're a Little Fucker, you're an Intermediary Fucker, and then—unless there's a glandular problem—you'll be a Big Fucker. It's just geometry!

I thought, "Wow! If they're going to persecute me just for saying what I'm going to physically be, maybe it's a good thing I didn't tell them about . . . the *Communism* stuff."

And that's when I got my first inkling of the tactic my mom called "boring from within"—which on the Left has an unfortunate double meaning. But what it's *supposed* to mean is that—instead of proclaiming yourself to the masses, as I had done—you take them aside, one by one, inculcating in each your political values, until you develop this loyal cadre, this revolutionary vanguard.

Then—with your revolutionary cadre in place—*then* you can lead the masses.

I tried this during recess: "Jimmy, Edie, Juan, Pedro . . . Björn . . . Who are we? . . . We are the young; we are the small; we are the weak—we are the kindergarteners. And who are our enemies? They are the old, the large, the cruel—they are the first-graders.

"Comrades, we are engaged in what my parents would call

a class struggle. And we cannot go about fighting this as individuals.

"Let me show you why:

"Take this twig. One of us alone is like this twig. A first-grader wants to bend this twig—easy—it breaks. But just imagine I had two twigs—that's two of us—much harder to break. Three twigs—even harder. And . . . whatever comes after three, even harder."

But instead of developing a small revolutionary cadre about me, I ended up getting beaten up with a frightening regularity—by what I now realize were the *lumpen* element of my kindergarten class.

It got to the point where Mrs. Spielhagen was so concerned that she called in my parents from their opposite ends of Manhattan—my father from the Lower East Side and my mother from nearby in Washington Heights. Mrs. Spielhagen told them, "Get your son out of public school before he is killed! This will certainly happen by middle school, so hurry."

My parents agreed this was a priority. They did intensive research together on what would be the best private school to send me to. And the private school they picked to send me to was the Cathedral School of St. John the Divine.

Now, it may sound like an odd choice, for my parents to send their Communistic, atheistic, Jewish-istic son to an all-boys Episcopalian choir school—but to them it made sense. Especially to my dad, because my dad was really into Jesus—not, of course, as the Son of God or anything, but Jesus as a nice Jewish revolutionary guy: thin, in good shape, with a nice beard . . . A great fucker—my dad said it was documented!

And I did enjoy singing in the choir—it turned out me and my dad had sung a lot of those hymns going downhill. What got to me were the sermons. Sure, the ministers talked a lot about Jesus, but they almost never focused on his revolutionariness, his Jewishness, his Big Fuckerdom; to me, his salient qualities were being virtually ignored. I mean, sometimes they even seemed to be treating him like some kind of a . . . deity!

After a couple weeks of this, I just couldn't take it anymore. I ran home to my mom. I said, "Mom, I know you and Dad need me to be in the choir so we can have this choir scholarship so you can afford to send me to private school so I don't get killed in public school. But Mom, you have no idea how much religion is going on in that church! Please, can I leave the choir?"

My mom, as always, inska in her response. She said, "Now Josh, first of all, it's 'May I leave the choir?' No, you may not. I want you to relax, go back to the choir, and every time they make you cross yourself, just say, under your breath, 'There—Is—No—God.'"

And in saying that over and over, I was able to stay centered in my faith.

It was a real victory for the inska approach to problem solving. My father took it as a defeat: he had been advocating the more ouska approach of my physically attacking the choirmaster in his sleep.

This was around the time Dad decided he was losing influence over me; he felt isolated all the way down there on the Lower East Side. Dad decided he wanted to move up closer to my mom, so that I could go back and forth more easily, and thus end up spending more time with Dad since he was such a cool guy. But I guess he was afraid that if he made the move all at once, Mom would notice and move away. So Dad developed this plan: he started moving six, seven blocks at a time—just trying to sneak up Manhattan on my mom, hoping she wouldn't notice. But my mom, of course, a very perceptive woman . . . I'm sure on the back of some closet door she had a map of Manhattan with pins: "He's at Fourteenth Street; he's at Twenty-third Street . . ."

And of course, Dad wasn't exactly being discreet, either. Everywhere he was moving, he was naked, he was knocking down walls, his hair was flying, his beard was billowing, he was yelling, he was singing . . . These songs were like the call of the wild for other like-minded Communist folksingers. Dad attracted them to him as he moved north up the island—and by the time he arrived at West Eighty-fourth Street (about halfway up), he had around him the minimum necessary number—the minyan—of Communist folksingers you need to form . . . a hootenanny.

A hootenanny, technically, of course, is a sing-along—but in the case of my dad and his friends, you'd sing a song, then have a political argument, then sing another song, then have another political argument . . . on and on, in strict alternation.

There was Marshall García, my father's childhood friend from the Bronx. Of all the Communists who came to the hootenannies,

Marshall was the only one who actually went to meetings of the Communist Party. And he resented that. He figured all these other so-called Communists were out having their fun, and he was left to be, like, the designated driver of the Revolution:

"Comrades, comrades, I don't mean to point fingers, but in the past several weeks I have not seen a single one of you at meetings of the local Party club. Need I remind you, comrades, that as hard as it may be to live *inside* the Party, it's even harder to live *outside* the Party."

And everyone would leap up and denounce the Communist Party as this sclerotic organization that had betrayed the original ideals of Marx and Engels and Lenin. Yelling and screaming—and then Chuck Yerkes would sing, *"Yo soy un hombre sincero . . ."* And we'd all go, *"De donde crece la palma . . ."* And Marshall would sit down, and it would be Chuck's turn.

The Reverend Chuck Yerkes was a tall, handsome Marxist Presbyterian minister who for years had worked in the prison ministry—until he was fired for handing out McDonald's straws to prisoners that said, "You Deserve a Break Today." Chuck would go, "Now people, I know I'm not going to convert you overnight to my belief in that Big Daddy up there. But if I could remind you that many of these songs we sing are drawn from the religious tradition I represent. So if you could think of adding a little spiritual flavor to your revolutionary fervor."

And everyone would leap up and denounce religion as the opiate of the masses—there's yelling and screaming—and Sam Vogel would get up and sing,

Tum-bala, tum-bala, tum-balalaika
Tum-bala, tum-bala, tum-balalaika . . .

Sam was the most ferocious-looking of the hootenanniers. He was barrel-chested, and he'd shaved his head bald. Very fierce-looking, but he loved singing these delicate little traditional Jewish songs, like:

Tum-balalaika, shpil balalaika
Tum-balalaika, freylech zol zayn.

"Play the balalaika and we'll all be happy." We'd all sing along happily with Sam—and at the end of the song Sam Vogel would turn to my father, who'd be sitting happily in his armchair, and Sam would go, "Paul, you're an anti-Semite!"

Which I know sounds like it was coming out of nowhere. But everyone at the hootenanny knew it was just part of Sam and Dad's running argument about Israel. Sam was for it; my father was against it. And I'm not oversimplifying. I'm giving you their argument in its full complexity! I may even have added a layer!

My father wouldn't take offense. No, this happened every hootenanny. He'd smile up at Sam and say, "But Sam, I'm Jewish!"

"But Paul, you're an anti-Semite!"

"But I'm Jewish!"

"But you're an anti-Semite!"

"But I'm Jewish!"

"But you're an anti-Semite!"

You could go out for coffee and come back; it would still be going on.

Fortunately, around this time an ameliorating influence came into our lives: Sue. Sue Kover. Suzanne Rose Kover. Just off the bus from Ottawa Lake, Michigan—a tiny town, population about 45. Sue and Dad met as teachers in adjacent classrooms, then they started dating, then Sue became my stepmother, and then Dad and Sue had the children who are my brothers and my sister.

Sue was an anomaly in our family. Unlike everyone else, Sue was not Jewish, not a New Yorker, not a City College grad, not a Communist . . . In other words: an oddball.

But she was so direct. You could ask her, "What's for dinner tonight?" With my parents it would be: "Well, in the feudal system, food was distributed—" With Sue you'd ask, "What's for dinner tonight?"

And she'd answer, "Meat."

And that's what it was; it was a big chunk of "meat." She'd put it in a pressure cooker and she'd serve it and, I mean, I don't think she added anything; it was delicious, but it was just "meat." I mean, she just put it in this pot, took it out, it was "meat." I mean, if you saw it, you'd go, "Meat." If you took Vladimir Nabokov back from the grave and pushed him up to the table and said, "Vladimir, bring your full vocabulary to bear on what you see before you," he'd go, "Meat."

I thought someone with this direct an approach towards food

might have a similarly direct approach towards sex. Which was a matter of some urgency to me as I approached my high school years. After spending all that time at an all-boys Episcopalian choir school, in a few weeks I was off to high school. And not just any high school—the Bronx High School of Science. You could tell from the name: party school. And I wanted to be ready.

So one day I pulled Sue aside. I said, "Sue, please don't tell Dad I'm still confused about this stuff, but as you know I'm about to go off to high school and there's going to be girls there. Could you tell me in your simple, direct way: How does sex work?"

She said, "Oh, you'll find out."

I said, "No, I need to know."

She said, "Okay . . ."

And this is what she told me—as far as I can remember, word for word. She said, "The man puts his penis inside the woman. The man goes in and out, in and out, in and out. The man and the woman get happier and happier and happier. And then the man and the woman have . . . an orgasm!" (By the way, I still keep that list by my bed—because you don't want to get happier out of order, in my experience; it can throw everyone off.)

She started to walk away. I said, "Wait, Sue, wait! What's this *orgasm* thing? It seems very important!"

She said, "Oh, you'll find out."

I said, "No, I need to know."

She said, "Well, the closest thing I can think of is, an orgasm is kind of like . . . a sneeze."

A sneeze! *A sneeze!* Then I'm being groomed to be a Big . . .
Sneezer?

This stuff was getting way too confusing. I was going to have
to go to the ultimate authority in my family: my mom's dad, the
oldest living member of our family, Julius Selden—the Oracle
of 140th Street. Grandpa and Grandma met each other on the
boat coming over from Russia, and when they got to the United
States, they became Communists. . . . Let me run that back for
you: they left Russia; they got on a boat; and then, when they arrived here—*then* they became Communists. Timing is everything!
. . . And Grandpa was reputed to have been an incredible
swinger back in the *shtetl*—so he seemed like the obvious person
to go to.

The only problem with asking Grandpa's advice is that he's
never been that *linear.* More of a storyteller, my grandpa. Like
when I was little and I used to stay over at Grandma and Grandpa's, they would tuck me in the bed that had been my mom's bed
when she was a little girl, and Grandpa would sit down on the
side of the bed and tell me this story:

"A little boy goes to the candy store. Man behind the counter
goes, 'Whaddaya want?' Boy goes, 'Whaddaya got?' Man
goes, 'Whaddaya want?' Boy goes, 'Whaddaya got?' Man goes,
'Whaddaya want?' Boy goes, 'Whaddaya got?'. . ."

That's the whole story. . . . He'd just keep saying that, over
and over—until I fell asleep.

So when I heard that Grandpa was at work on a *novel,* there were some concerns in my mind—like about plot throughline, or character development . . .

But I had no one else to ask, so the week before I went off to high school I went up to Grandpa and I said, "Please, Grandpa, share with me your age-old wisdom on how to deal with girls."

And what he said to me was, "Stay away from girls, so you can focus on your work."

Thank you, Grandpa.

Armed with that very useful advice, I went off to high school that first day, hoping that I was going to be instantly immersed in teen culture. I'd be a teen embraced by teen culture.

I got to Bronx Science; I walked in. All around me, I saw, immediately, teen culture. The problem was, I was not a part of it. I could see the teens who were in teen culture—they were kissing, touching, holding hands. They were kids who were integrated in some fundamental sense with their bodies; I would call them "body-people." And I realized that day that I was not a body-person; what I was, I realized, was . . . a *head*—a head that is carried about on this vestigial organ called my *body*, which would carry my head around on this sort of ectoplasmic ooze from class to class, from which vantage point my head could observe the body-people and their doings. I never had a date: I couldn't get close enough to a girl—my ooze would precede me.

Really, the closest I got to sex—even on a theoretical level—in those days was through listening in on my mom's writers' workshops.

My mom had these writers' workshops; they would gather

in our living room every week. The only criterion for being in my mom's writers' workshops was that your work be . . . un-publishable.

So they'd gather in our living room and read from their un-publishable works, which were invariably erotic in nature. And even though I was lying in my bed, I could hear every word, be-cause—going way up into my teens—my mom still would not let me have a door to my room.

So the words would come floating in from my mom and her friends—like Ruth Goldberg. Who would have imagined the erot-icism lurking inside Ruth Goldberg, a woman who wore earth tones, oranges and browns, capes and berets—and spoke with this HIGH PIERCING VOICE?

Ruth's erotic adventures tended to take place at: MACY'S . . . GIMBEL'S . . . when it got kinky—F·A·O SCHWARZ.

Or Sy Paskoff! In his glory years, Sy had been president of the Heights-Inwood Reform Democratic Club. But that had been the pinnacle for him. Since then, Sy had done several decades of hard labor as a guidance counselor in the New York public school system. As a result, Sy now hated all children—all *people*, really. A shriveled, wizened, desiccated little guy. (I'm sure at one point he used to be very tall and handsome and willowy, but now . . .) He had these thick, black-framed glasses, with thick lenses. According to my mom, Sy Paskoff never took buses, be-cause *people* were on them; and—again, according to my mom—Sy took sleeping pills during the day—just to keep going!

"I'd like to read from my latest chapter," Sy would begin.

"She stood before me. Glistening. With what? WHAT? Sweat? Tears? WHAT?" He turned the page. "WHAT?"

Or my mom, Bunny. For months she had been working on this teen romance. It involved these two young teen scientists—a boy and a girl—and they're working in their high-school laboratory . . . and independently they discover that when you rub Clearasil on a nuclear warhead, it deactivates it.

I remember when my mom finally read to the workshop from the first chapter of "Sci-Fi High." I was lying in my bed, and the words from her chapter came floating in through my open doorway. And right away I realized that the lead hunk, the male hero dude of my mom's teen romance—was named . . . "Josh." "Kornbluth."

So I had to get myself out of bed, and I made my way through the kitchen and looked out from the kitchen doorway into the living room.

"Uh, excuse me, Mom? Um . . . um . . . 'Josh,' I could see, maybe. 'Josh.' But why 'Josh Kornbluth'? Why 'Josh . . . Kornbluth'?"

She said, "Oh honey, you know I have trouble thinking up names. Go back to sleep."

"Okay."

And I drifted back to my room—as people were wont to do, during breaks between chapter-readings, because there was no door separating the kitchen from my room, and all the cabinets of cans extended from the kitchen into my room. During breaks people would follow the cabinets of cans into my room, looking for, like, maraschino cherries or something. And then at some point they would notice, shrouded in the darkness, the huddled, overweight, adolescent male figure lying there. And they would go, "Oh!"

And often I would have *just* drifted off to sleep, so I'd wake up to: "Oh!" I'd see this embarrassed silhouette go creeping out—and go back to reading from their erotic works.

But one night, during a workshop, I had just drifted off to sleep when I awoke to a new "Oh!"

I looked—and I saw this new silhouette. Abundant! . . . Hair! Lots of hair. And breasts! (Just two, but . . .)

And the silhouette said, "Oh!" and drifted out of my room.

Well, I had to follow to see who this new silhouette belonged to. I looked out through the kitchen doorway into the living room . . . and there she was! She was on the couch. Her legs were crossed. She was crocheting. Black hair—*black* hair. And freckles. And this kind of pessimistic sort of smile.

And as I watched her, Sy Paskoff turned to this beauty and went, "Marcie, you're new here. What do you have to read to us? WHAT?"

She said, "Oh, I'm happy just listening. Go ahead."

I thought, "Marcie. *Marcie.* Her name's Marcie! . . . Josh and Marcie . . . Marcie and Josh . . . leading the Revolution. It could work. She could be my *Pasionaria;* I could be her . . . *Pasionario.* . . . I have to meet her; I have to meet this woman."

So during the next break, I walked out into the living room until I was standing right in front of where Marcie was sitting on the couch.

"Hi, Marcie. I'm Bunny's son, Josh. . . . Right, 'Josh Kornbluth.' And I was just wondering . . . uh . . . if you would give me . . . crocheting lessons."

And she looked up at me and asked (I think reasonably), "Why?"

I had to think on my feet at that point. I was playing a lot of oboe at the time, so I said: "Well, the winter is coming. It's getting cold. I'll need to make a case for my oboe."

"A case for your oboe."

"Yeah, to keep it . . . warm."

"Josh, can I tell you something?"

"Sure. What?"

"You have your mother's eyes."

"Uh, thanks. . . . Thanks."

And the day of my first crocheting lesson finally arrived! I ran the few blocks to Marcie's building. I ran into her building. I got onto the elevator. I pressed "6" for the top floor, Marcie's floor. The door shut, there was a lurch, and the elevator started to move up—incredibly slowly.

It was a very old elevator—possibly the original elevator made by Otis when he was a little boy . . . for, like, a school project. It even said, in crayon, "Otis." From underneath I could hear squeaking, which I imagined was the gerbil in the wheel, powering the vehicle. And there was this crudely cut diamond-shaped window in the front, so you could watch in early Diamond Vision as the floors went oozing by: "1 . . . 2 . . . 3 . . ." You know, denoting the number of years that had passed since you'd gotten on the elevator.

And then, finally, "6"! I got off the elevator, looked for 6-H—and as I was running down the hallway to 6-H, I passed this apartment where someone was obviously frying plantains, and I *love* fried plantains, but . . . no! I ran up to 6-H; I rang the buzzer.

Footsteps. The door opened. And there she was! With her freckles, and her smile, and her black hair—and behind her this kind of . . . halo? I mean, it turns out it was the kitchen behind her; it was painted bright yellow and brightly lit, but for a second it looked, you know, just like a . . .

Okay. So there we were, in Marcie's dilapidated living room. I'm sitting next to her on the couch, having my first-ever crocheting lesson.

It would have been perfect—perfect!—if we had only been . . . alone. But there was her husband, Morty, right next to the couch, sort of lurking around, scratching his scraggly beard. (I know it was his apartment, too—they were married; it's communal property, or whatever—but there was something loitering-esque in the way he was just *slouching* there.)

So there's the husband, Morty; and then there's the dog, Beanie. As much as I lusted for Marcie, Beanie lusted easily as much . . . for my leg. One of *those* dogs. A snooty, snouty, pointy-nosed little dog. Maybe not even a dog—maybe a rat. Maybe on the rat/dog cusp of evolution. (I mean, he had the pointy nose, the beady eyes, the buckteeth, the whiskers—so, *technically* a dog, but . . .)

And it was hard enough trying to crochet for the first time while sitting next to this beautiful woman. But then to have to also fend off Beanie's constant advances, while not seeming to be . . . evil. Very difficult.

But it got worse. Beanie started coming at me in waves—and I'm fending him off, fending him off. Finally I decided: I just have to give Beanie one big swat; I just have to give Beanie one big swat. So I reared my hand back to give Beanie one big swat . . . evidently just at the moment that Marcie was taking a sip of water from a glass. And my hand hit the glass, and it splashed water onto her shirt—directly over her left breast.

I looked at her. Mortified, yet aroused. A combination I've stuck with.

But Marcie was just calmly wiping the water off her shirt—just smooshing off the water. Then at some point she noticed my stare. She said, "Oh, Josh, don't worry. It's only water. And anyhow, you know my last name, don't you? It's 'Wasserman.' That makes me a 'Water-Person.' And anyhow, you're so young. You probably think these accidents all have permanent ramifications. But when you get older, you'll see: more often than not, the ramifications are not permanent. No. More often than not, the ramifications are, mmmmm . . ."

I said, *"Ephemeral?"*

"Yeah, *ephemeral*. I like that word. . . . You know, Josh, I love words so much; I think that's why I've never finished writing a story. I get so infatuated with each individual word that even a paragraph starts to look . . . obscene."

I caught her stare; and then I followed her stare as it left me— I followed it up, up, up . . . to . . . Morty, scowling down.

By this point my dad had finally accomplished his long-standing goal of moving close to my mom. In fact, in his exuberance he'd actually overshot my mom by eleven blocks. (Whoa!) And Dad and Sue had started to have a new family: Jacob and Amy were really little (I don't think Sammy had been born yet).

And as the months went by with Marcie, my crocheting was proceeding apace. The only problem was, I had way too much material for an oboe case. So I was making up these excuses: "Uh, bassoon case!"

And at school, filled with a new libidinous energy from being around Marcie so much, I got all the other members of the Bronx Science Marxist-Leninist Study Group to agree to spend the next summer on a historic trip to the Soviet Union . . . although, as it turned out, we had to hook up with a larger group of high-school students from all around the country because we couldn't find good rates for just the three of us.

And at Marcie's I had crocheted even more material: "Uh . . . tuba case!"

And at school I seized control of the Marxist-Leninist Study Group, causing the other two members to quit. So now I was not just the commissar but also the rank-and-file—which was a drag, because I'd been preparing to deliver this speech to them on "The Nature of Dialectics."

And at Marcie's, I had *way* too much material: "Uh . . . orchestra case!"

Mom said she was worried that I might not dress warmly enough in Russia. But I assured her, "Look, I'm doing all this crocheting—"

Crocheting! Wait—I hadn't told Marcie about my trip yet. And it was only a few days away! I should drop in on her and tell her. I'd never dropped in on her during a non–regularly-scheduled-crocheting-lesson day, but I was sure she'd be glad to see me.

I ran to Marcie's building, got onto the elevator, pressed "6," the door shut, there was a lurch—and as the elevator ascended with its typical glaciosity, I had a chance to rehearse:

"Hi, Marcie, it's me—Josh." No, that's stupid—she knows it's me . . .

"Hi, Marcie, I just wanted to tell you that the reason I've been crocheting is that I really like you and I don't actually care about crocheting and I'm going to Russia and I'd like you to come with me . . ." Too much information.

"I luff you! I luff you, and you luff me! You will come away with me—to Russia! Ngrrrh! Over the tundra! Leave Morrrh . . .

Beanhhh . . . Rrrrr mmmmmm—" Well, perhaps that's a tad on the guttural side, but I think I'm on the right track. I mean, she likes me; she definitely likes me; maybe she loves me; maybe she even . . . *lusts* for me.

Finally: 6!

I got off the elevator—and as I was running down the hallway to 6-H, I passed the apartment with the frying plantains, but . . . no! And I went up to 6-H, and I was just about to press the buzzer, when I heard . . . shouting. Shouting from the back of 6-H. It was Marcie's voice, yelling. And Morty, too—yelling.

Maybe this is a bad time. Maybe I should come back some other— No. The time is now!

I rang the bell. The shouting stopped. Silence—then footsteps. The door opened—but just a crack. In the crack of the doorway: Marcie. Behind her—looming—Morty.

Marcie said, "Josh, what are you doing here? We don't have a lesson scheduled today. Don't you call in advance before you come over to a place? Don't you have any manners? We're busy now, Josh. We don't need you here. Go away. Go *away!*"

And she slammed the door shut.

Oh. I've evidently miscalculated. I was having a big fantasy-head. I was imagining me with Marcie. And I'm just a kid, and she's, like, a grown woman, she's a beautiful grown woman, and she's married. I've done something wrong. I've broken the fabric, and I don't know if I can fix it. . . .

Comrades, the nature of dialectics is often misunderstood. Dialectical change, though it will lead to a shining Utopia—dialectical change has nothing to do with love . . . and everything to do with conflict. Through conflict—through suffering—that's how we move forward, through the bleak times, to a glorious future in which totally opposing forces inevitably—paradoxically—magically—become one.

The day I got back from the Soviet Union, everyone at the hootenanny was singing "Guantanamera," when my dad said:

"All right, everyone, be quiet, please—be quiet! Enough singing. Please sit down . . . sit ouska-down! Sam, Marshall, Chuck, everyone, please sit down. . . . We have a young man here, just back from his trip to the Soviet Union, waiting to share with us his—I'm sure—exciting stories. So let us all now listen attentively to my son as he describes to us his—I'm sure—revolutionary experiences in the Land of Socialism."

"Thanks, Dad.

"*The Soviet Union and What It Meant to Me.* . . . It was vast. Vast. You know, you see it on a map and it's about *that* big, and you go there and it's way bigger. Vast. . . . And the colors don't change when you cross borders, like on a map. It's drab. *Drab.* Vast and drab. . . .

"Oh, a *good* kind of drab, Dad. You know, we're used to thinking of drabness as a negative trait. But you go there, and you see a new kind of drabness—a revolutionary drabness. And underneath the drabness, you can sense the roiling—the roiling of a people still at work on the Revolution.

"Roiling . . . Even we—almost as soon as we got off the plane—we, too, were roiling. And it wasn't just the food. It was the sense of the Revolution that was going on all around us.

"Oh, and to see the hospitals! The socialist health care—which of course you need, for all the roiling. You can go in and sort of unroil, and then you can go out and see the banners . . .

"The banners! Oh, you have not seen Brezhnev. You may think you've seen him, if you've seen him on TV, or even live . . . But you have not seen Brezhnev until you have seen him on a banner, *one acre.* Just the head of Brezhnev, one acre. A mole on Brezhnev—yea big! Pores on the man, huge pimples and abrasions . . . I mean, clearly the leadership is not hogging the skincare products. Nivea has not trickled up to the Kremlin . . .

"Oh, and we saw Lenin himself. Lenin! We saw the man himself in his tomb, under glass. Oh Dad, yeah, they love him, they love him there. They wait in long lines to see Lenin—long, drab lines to see Lenin. I'm sure some of them think it's *bread*—but once they get there and realize that it's Lenin, I'm sure their excitement would be what I felt. I mean, he looks so good—a little waxy, but good, very confident, very serene. Not like what we'd do in America: we'd Disney-fy him, have an animatronic Lenin. 'Hello, kiddies! I'm Vlady Lenin. How are you enjoying the Revolution? It's a Red World After All! Put in another kopeck . . . kopeck . . . kopeck . . .' None of that—

"Sorry—what, Marshall? Oh right, yeah. . . . The meetings in the Soviet Union are very well attended. I promised Marshall I'd tell you that. I mean, we didn't actually go to any meetings, but I'm sure—

"Oh, and Chuck! We went to that church you were worried about. No need to worry—it's in great shape. They turned it into a museum, so it's nice and clean; it doesn't have those scuff-marks from people actually *worshipping* there—

"What, Sam? . . . Yes, of course there are synagogues there, Sam. I was just telling Chuck about this church. Wait, wait, wait, Sam—I am not trying to reject my heritage, Sam! I didn't *resist* seeing any synagogues—they just didn't take us to—

"Dad, I can handle this—

"Sam, why would I not want to go to a synagogue? . . . But Sam, I'm Jewish! . . . But I'm Jewish! . . . But I'm Jewish! . . .

"Look, would everyone just stop yelling at each other and sit down?"

It was no use. They'd gone too long at a hootenanny without arguing with each other. They had to blow off steam for a while. So while they're all yelling, let me tell you what *really* happened to me in the Land of Socialism. . . .

They put us on the overnight train to Kiev. They told us they were sending us to this little camp for medical students in the Ukraine. (Why send us American high-school students to a camp for medical students, we didn't know. But we figured, well, if we need ointment or Band-Aids, they'll have them there . . .)

So we're on this long, drab overnight train to Kiev. Two of us per compartment. We were thrown in together randomly. And I was thrown in together randomly with Luellen—the prettiest girl in our group.

Luellen. I knew she was special, because right when she walked into my compartment, my hand instinctively reached for a crochet hook. But this wasn't Marcie; this was Luellen. Blond, and smiling . . . and sitting down next to me on the bottom berth as we set off on the overnight trip to Kiev.

"Hi, Luellen—I'm Josh. I know none of us really had a chance to talk on the Aeroflot plane coming over. Are you here because you are, like me, a red diaper baby?"

"Huh?"

"Are you here because your parents are Communists?"

"What?"

"I'm sorry; I'm being too general. Are your parents . . . Stalinists? Are they . . . Trotskyites?"

"They're . . . socialites!"

"Oh, yeah, I remember when they broke off from the PLP; it was very bloody. . . . Well, I'm sure there must be *some* similarities. Like, I guess you guys, you played, I assume, Monopoly as a family? Yeah, well, we did too. I don't know if you've played Monopoly with Communists, but it's very frustrating. Everyone wants to go into jail, to make a political statement. Grandma would go into jail and wage a hunger strike; she'd refuse to come out: 'Free Parking for Everyone!' Grandpa would nationalize the railroads. I would play by the rules; I would win Park Place and put up some hotels, some buildings. Then at some point, I'd have to leave the room and go make a wee-wee. While I was away, my mom would organize the tenants on Park Place into a rent strike. Little tokens would be circling my property! When I came back, my grandma would be yelling at me, 'Scab! Scab! Scab!'

"No, no, I wasn't *bleeding*, Luellen. 'Scab' is a term that means—"

Luckily, just then the door was flung open and in came the porter with this big tray filled with bottles and glasses and . . . grapes! I hadn't eaten grapes in years! "Wait, are these grapes okay? No, Chavez can't be boycotting these grapes. Luellen, we can eat these! You know about the boycott, the UFW? . . . Never mind, let's just eat the grapes. . . .

"Porter, is this *vodka* in these bottles?"

No, the porter told me—what was in the bottles was *better* than vodka; it was grain alcohol, three billion proof. And the porter told me: very important—after every sip of grain alcohol, you must have a little bite of bread from the bread basket. Otherwise, he said, the alcohol is so strong, "you'll go blind!"

"Thank you. All I have is this twenty-kopeck note. Why don't you keep two kopecks and give me back—" He took my twenty-kopeck note and disappeared. Oh, I guess he'll share it with all the other porters in the Soviet Union . . .

"So Luellen, would you like some . . . ? Great!"

I poured us some grain alcohol. And we rattled off towards Kiev on our overnight train, sipping grain alcohol and eating little bites of bread. It's a good thing we had the bread, because I wasn't used to drinking—and even with the bread I didn't go blind, but my eyes did dilate. In fact, my whole body dilated . . . And at some point I drifted off to sleep.

During the night, as I slept—alone—in the bottom berth, I had a dream. In my dream, I was trying to enter a beautiful new country: the Land of Luellen. I was stopped at the border guard's booth. The border guard came out—turned out to be Marcie, wearing a crocheted halter top. And now I'm inside the Land of Luellen. But I don't see any Luellens around. Then I realized that in my hands was my *oboe*, for some reason. So I started to play it, and little Luellens started sprouting out of the ground, little blond Luellens dancing around me as I played my oboe higher and higher, higher and higher, until I hit my highest note—and just then all the Luellens simultaneously . . . sneezed!

And I woke up. And just upon waking I realized that in the moments just *before* waking, something had happened . . . in my pants. Something nocturnal and unwanted.

Oh, and we're pulling into the Kiev station! I don't have time to change!

I ran up to the window to check things out, pantswise: I couldn't see anything—it must have all evaporated or something. I said, "Thank you, God. I don't believe in you, but I'm a friend of Chuck's. Thank you!"

As I was about to step down from the train car, Luellen appeared next to me. She had changed into a nice-looking peasant shirt. It was the only peasant shirt I'd ever seen that said "Dior"—

but otherwise, very authentic looking. And as we stepped down from the train, Luellen looked at me, smiled, and said, "So Josh, I see you're growing a beard."

She was right! I hadn't been the day before. I thought, "Wow—that Soviet moonshine!"

Finally, we arrived at our little camp. We could see the welcoming party of Soviet medical students waiting to greet us in the distance. But before we went to meet them, I wanted to have a little word with the other kids in my group. Because from listening in on their conversations on the bus coming in from the train station, I'd gotten the sense that none of them were red diaper babies like me. So before they made fools of themselves with our Soviet hosts, I wanted to have a little chat with them:

"Excuse me . . . Biff, Chip, Maitlin, Caitlin, Whitney . . . Houston . . . Björn . . . I know none of you care about socialism; I know none of you care about the Soviet Union. I figure you're all wealthy American teens who've been everywhere else on earth *except* the Soviet Union; I figure you've come here so that before college you can achieve global closure.

"And I know that if you all had your druthers, you'd go running right down to the beach and spend the summer hanging out there by the River Dnieper.

"But I want you to know: you have a choice. You can go down to the beach, and thus experience the beach . . . *or* you can hang out with me and experience socialism. Okay? It's your choice: the beach, or socialism. . . .

"Well, I hope you all enjoy yourselves! . . . I'm gonna go meet some young Soviets; that's why *I* came here. . . .

"*Sdrastveetsyeh! Minya zavoot* Josh—*noh tsebyeh minya zavoot Yasha!*" (The reason I went to Bronx Science instead of Stuyvesant is that Stuyvesant did not offer Russian.) "*Ya Amerikanskee Commooneest! Ya Amerikanskee Commooneest!* . . . *Mozhet bueets:* Gus Hall!

"*Ya oychen radt—Sahvyetskee Sahyuz—AAH! Sahtseeyaleezm—AAH! Commooneezm—AAH!* . . . *Amereeka—PTEH! Capeetaleezm—PTEH!* Beach—*PTEH!* . . . *Ya Amerikanskee Commooneest! Vui Sahvyetskee Commoonneestee! Zdrastveetsyeh, tahvahrishchee!*"

The young Soviets all listened to me politely. And when I was done, one of them leaned forward and went, "Geeve us your blue jeans."

"What? You want my *pants?* What do you want with my pants? . . . Well, first of all, you don't want *these* pants. . . . But why do you want pants at all?"

"Choong gum!"

"Chewing gum? What's the big deal about chewing gum?"

"Pink Floyt!"

"You like Pink Floyd here?"

"John Denver!"

"You like John Denver here?"

One of the Ukrainian medical students even went, "Far-r-r fucking out!"

I thought, "What's going on here? The Soviet young people are more like the American young people than they're like me! I am evidently an anomaly of Earth!"

When we got back to JFK—or, as my father called it, "The Bay of Pigs Memorial Airport"—I couldn't wait to be reunited with my dad and show off my new beard. We'd be two bearded guys now! And I was just about to go down the escalator to the baggage claim when I heard the familiar "Hey, Fucker!"

I looked, and I saw this man coming towards me. The potbelly seemed familiar, but the man coming towards me did not have a beard—he was clean shaven. And he didn't have long, straggly hair—he had short hair. And he wasn't wearing a bright orange jumpsuit—he was wearing a *suit* suit . . . not a real *expensive*-looking suit, but a suit.

The man came up to me and he hugged me, and I thought, "Well, this must be my dad—but what gives?"

On the car ride back into Manhattan, he explained:

While I had been away in the Soviet Union, Dad had gotten a new job. By this point, the radius away from New York he had to go to be licensed to teach had extended to about two hours. He'd finally found a job in Stamford, Connecticut—at the Cloonan Middle School.

But this job was going to be different. Because my father . . . usually he was this lone voice raging against the system—but now, at Cloonan, he was going to have his dream job: he was going to lead a project. He would handpick three other teachers for this project, and together, Dad and these teachers were going to take the bottom four classes entering the seventh grade at Cloonan.

All these kids were illiterate—all of them. Many of them could not recite the alphabet. My father was going to show that, as he put it, all these children had learned is that they could not learn. And he would show that that wasn't true. Using love, and discipline—and phonetics—he would take these kids, illiterate at the beginning of the seventh grade, and by the end of the eighth grade he would have them reading *The Grapes of Wrath*. (Well, what did you think he was going to have them read? *Atlas Shrugged?*)

Dad told me that when we got back to the apartment—on what would ordinarily be hootenanny night—instead, in my honor, the hootenanny would be devoted to me telling of my revolutionary experiences in the Land of Socialism.

As I walked back to my mom's that evening, I felt bad: I hadn't given the hootenanniers the Soviet experience they'd wanted.

When I got back to my mom's apartment, I went into my room—and saw in the corner this big pile of material I'd crocheted that I'd never known what to do with. . . . I picked up the material, and I pinned it up over my doorway. I had crocheted a door to my room!

A few days later I got a call. It was Marcie.

She said, "Josh, can you come over right away? We need to talk."

Well, we obviously hadn't scheduled a crocheting lesson. I said, "Should I bring my hook . . . and my yarn?"

She said, "Don't bother."

As I walked through the neighborhood without my hook and my yarn, my hands felt naked, weightless.

I walked into the building, got onto the elevator, pressed "6," the door started to shut . . . And for once I was so glad that this was an incredibly slow elevator. In fact, maybe if I'm lucky it'll be *infinitely* slow, and I'll never reach the sixth floor.

Because I was starting to picture the scenario: I'd get off at the sixth floor, I'd go down the hallway, I'd ring the buzzer, the door would open, and standing there in the doorway would be . . . Marcie—and, next to her, . . . Morty. And Marcie's gonna go, "Josh, I just wanted to tell you: I've seen through you all along. You disgust me. But thanks for dropping by." And Morty's gonna go, "You little *putz*—"

And the door shut, there was a lurch, and the elevator started to go up—incredibly fast! . . . 1! 2! 3! It was like someone had fed speed to the gerbils, or something. . . . 4! "No!" 5! "No!" 6! "No!"

And I got off the elevator. And Marcie was standing there in the hallway, wearing only a pink chenille bathrobe. (I used to think it was terry cloth, but people have told me over and over that it was chenille—which is weird, since they weren't there.)

She said, "Josh, thanks for coming. Morty has left me. I'm alone. . . . I'm *alone*. . . . And the reason I invited you here is, it's a new phase in my life. I want to cut my hair. But I'm afraid to cut my own hair. Would *you* cut my hair?"

Well, I'd been taking this computer-logic class at school—in the BASIC language of computer. And we were doing these *If . . . then* trees. "If *a* is greater than *b,* then . . ." And you follow up all the ramifications. "If *a* is *less* than *b,* then . . ." And you follow up all *those* ramifications.

So I thought: "Okay. If I say, 'No, I won't cut your hair . . . Because, you know, I'm only seventeen, I love your hair, I've never cut hair—' *If* I say, 'No' . . . the *then:* limited. Limited, perhaps, to my previous experience. But if I say, 'Yes, I will cut your hair—' *If* I say, 'Yes' . . . the *then* branches out—who knows?"

So I said, "Yes, I will cut your hair." And as I followed Marcie towards her apartment, I could feel the *then* within me . . . rising.

I entered her apartment with my usual trepidation: you never knew where Beanie was going to pounce from.

I could see one beady eye and a little pointy snout from around the corner in the living room. And I had tried to perfect this way of entering Marcie's apartment without moving my legs, so I wouldn't excite Beanie. I slid into the kitchen that way. Marcie said, "Good. Why don't you sit down there? I'm going to take a shower, because it says you're supposed to get your hair . . . wet."

I sat down at the kitchen table, under the bright light and with the yellow paint all around, and I picked up this book she'd left there: *Haircutting: The Layer System.*

I tried to focus on the book, but I was having a hard time—because I could hear the shower water going in the bathroom. And in my mind I was picturing Marcie in the bathroom, taking off her pink chenille bathrobe, putting it up on a hook, and then—naked—getting into the bathtub, under the shower water.

And in my mind—I mean, she probably wasn't doing this—but in my mind I pictured her . . . spinning. With her breasts following slightly . . . behind.

I was trying to focus on the book, but the blood had left my brain. In fact, it had left all my extremities and was now going in this kind of reverse diaspora, towards—I don't know—Mesopotamia?

Beanie was eyeing me from the doorway; I eyed him back and tried to focus on the book.

But then the shower water stopped, and Marcie reemerged in the kitchen doorway. She was wearing her bathrobe, which was now clinging to her. Her black hair was glistening. Her skin was glowing.

I stood up—but I couldn't *totally;* so I tried to make it into this sort of . . . gallant gesture.

She sat down on the chair at the kitchen table. I walked around behind her and picked up a pair of scissors—as she bent down her head and said, "I totally trust you."

I began to cut. . . . It was working! Her hair was falling off! I don't think it was the layer system *precisely,* but hair was falling off. I could see a little pile of black hair forming on the linoleum, and I thought: "Well, maybe I should do the other side, too."

So I went around to the other side.

I watched the second pile of hair form on the linoleum, and

then overtake the first pile, and I thought: "Wait—I'm favoring this side, maybe because I'm left-handed."

So I went back around to the right side to compensate, but I kind of overcompensated, so I went back to the left side, and I overcompensated again. And now I started to panic a little bit, because I figured, intuitively: eventually, you must hit *head*—and you'd run out of room to maneuver.

But no matter what I tried, Marcie's hair was becoming increasingly lopsided—this Picasso-esque thing. So I just started snipping the scissors in the air, to stall for time. Then, in my panic, I started to hyperventilate. I thought, "Maybe I'm going to faint! Maybe I'm going to faint!"

And just to steady myself—to keep myself from fainting—I put my hand on her neck.

And when I put my hand on her neck, she craned her neck to the left.

So I switched the scissors to my other hand and put my other hand on the other side of her neck. And she craned her neck to the right.

So I put down the scissors, and I put both hands on both sides of her neck. And she tilted her head way back.

So I let my hands slide down her neck, around the top of her collar—till my fingertips were touching . . . I guess, her collarbone things? And I rubbed the skin over her collarbone things— and as I rubbed the skin there, I thought: "By rubbing her skin here, am I moving her breasts?"

I couldn't quite tell.

And I was trying to decide whether to pull open the front of her bathrobe.

I didn't want to make any sudden movements. I didn't want to break the spell; I didn't want to excite Beanie. Trying to decide whether to pull open the front of her bathrobe, when Marcie Wasserman . . . stood up! And she twirled around! And she hugged me! And she kissed me! Anth sthe shtuck her thongue in my mousth! . . . I'm sorry: she stuck her tongue in my mouth.

It's weird, you know—I hadn't anticipated the taste. I'd noticed that she was always smoking at the writers' workshops and at our crocheting lessons, but I hadn't anticipated the taste. Her tongue—it was ashy and hot. But her lips—it was weird—her lips were cold and wet. So it was like this cold, wet salamander with a hot, ashy worm—

I hope I'm not over-romanticizing.

And then she pulled back, and she said: "We probably shouldn't do this." Which, of course, although I had no way of knowing it at the time, every woman I'd ever go out with would say to me at some point. And then she struck a pose that I knew from paintings meant . . . to follow.

So I grabbed her hand, and she started pulling me across the living room, towards the bedroom. Beanie leapt up and attached to my leg; we were like the people with the Golden Goose!

Marcie whipped me into the bedroom. I kicked Beanie off. Marcie shut the double-doors, latched them, put a chair behind them. From behind the doors I could hear scratching. I thought: "Fuck you, Beanie—you're out of the loop!"

And now it was just me and Marcie Wasserman, alone in the Wassermanian bedroom.

Marcie was making her way to the huge double bed. Now she sat down on the bed, she leaned back, and she opened her bathrobe.

And there she was: her— Well, her hair. But her *face* was still symmetrical. And her freckles, and her neck, and her collarbone things, and . . . breasts! Rising and falling—possibly in some kind of coordination with her . . . breathing? Nipples—delineated against brown— I think I'd read in the *Playboy* "Advisor" they were called . . . "aereolies"? And her tummy, and—between her legs—this damp-looking, dark patch of—

I'd never seen it before. The only naked women I'd ever seen were in *Playboy*. And in *Playboy* at that time, there were naked women, of course, but they were naked from *here* down to *there,* and from *there* down. They'd always be behind . . . furniture. Because evidently there was a law at the time that if you were a naked woman in a photograph, you had to be near . . . furniture. Or a hedge.

So, out of habit, I briefly tried superimposing a chaise longue. But she was talking to me. She was saying: "Why don't you take off your clothes?"

I hadn't anticipated having to take off . . . my clothes. Underneath my clothes was . . . my body!

But she's looking at me, and she's waiting! Oh! . . . "If . . . then." . . . If I leave my shirt on . . . then: limited. If I take my shirt off . . . then: extended. I pulled off my shirt—and, sucking in my tummy, I started making my way towards Marcie.

She pointed out that I was still wearing my pants and my shoes. Noted; well taken.

I pulled off my sh— Oh, I can smell my sock from here! Oh, I can smell my other sock even worse! And there are holes in my socks, because I haven't cut my toenails!

I pulled off a sock, and then the other smelly sock—and then I undid my belt and started to pull down my pants—

And then I remembered my primal fear—my fear going back to when I was a little boy in gym class, in the locker room: my fear that my underpants might not look totally pristine, and someone might see them. So I became obsessed with pulling down my underpants with my pants, so Marcie would not see my underpants. And I pulled off my pants, and I covered my underpants with my pants . . .

I was so relieved that Marcie had not seen my underpants, I did not really think of the fact that I was now standing naked.

And I was *pointing* at her—so I followed myself to the bed and lay down next to Marcie.

She said, "Why don't you go . . . on top?"

"Okay."

I was on top of Marcie Wasserman.

She said, "Why don't you go . . . inside?"

"Okay."

"The man goes inside the woman"—yeah, it's on the list!

But it wasn't intuitively obvious—how to go inside. I kept bouncing off of something. I thought, "I must have the right region—it's the part that's hidden by . . . furniture." But how do I get in? I keep bouncing off. The man has to go inside the woman. The man doesn't bounce off the woman. The man goes inside the woman. This should be the easiest—

This should be the easiest thing in the *world* to do! I mean, how did we evolve all these billions of years? *Everything* can do this: coyotes can do this, Beanies can do this, protozoa— No, protozoa split. But mostly, everything can do this. Why can't *I* do this?

And I felt her hand on me, guiding me in. I thought, "Oh! We must have had . . . help!"

And now I was sliding in—slithering and sliding in. I felt like I was *miles* long, and I knew: I wasn't. Slithering and sliding in. I thought, "Of course I'm sliding in. Of course I'm sliding in. I'm a man! I'm a *man!* They're gonna name trees after me! I'll lead a revolution!"

Slithering and sliding in—and I slid all the way in. I remembered: the man goes in and out, in and out. But when I started to move inside her, Marcie started to . . . heave! And gasp! And her eyes rolled back! She started to froth!

I thought: "What is she *doing?* . . . Miss April never did this! Miss May never did this!"

Then I remembered: in hygiene class they'd just taught us about a certain condition some people get into where the important thing is to keep them from biting off . . . their tongue! I thought, "I have to keep her from biting off her tongue!"

But now I couldn't even think about her, because now she was heaving so much I was afraid of being thrown. I was holding onto the little lopsided fringes of hair left on her head. She was heaving. And now I was screaming—from vertigo. And Beanie's barking and throwing himself against the door: "Arf arf! Gotta save that leg! That leg is in trouble! Arf arf!"

He's barking, she's heaving, I'm screaming. Barking, heaving, screaming. And now something's happening to my penis! Something's happening to my penis! Wait! I understand revolutions now! The masses don't explode because they want to explode, they don't explode from political theory; they're like volcanoes—they explode because they can't *not* explo-o-ode! . . .

And I slid out.

And I looked up at Marcie, with I guess what must have been an expression of . . . triumph.

But she was looking down at me with a different look. Was it . . . consolatory?

She said, "That's okay, Josh—you don't have to feel . . . bad."

And that was the first moment it occurred to me that perhaps there was a reason I should feel . . . bad.

Oh: I probably should have stayed pointing longer. Evidently it's not enough in these situations simply to . . . survive.

And she was patting the pillow next to her. So I crawled up to the pillow, carrying with me my newfound sense of . . . insufficiency—a sense of insufficiency that would become a real pal in my adult life.

I got up to the pillow and I sank my head into the cool darkness. I just wanted to disappear! Just wanted to go away, dissolve into the pillow. I turned my head away from Marcie. I'm so embarrassed! I wasn't ready for this! I've disappointed her!

And cold air was blowing in through a crack in the window and ruffling my hair. Cold air was ruffling my hair. But then the air suddenly turned warm. It was Marcie's hand—she was stroking my hair!

She said: "Josh, it's okay. It happens. And you're young. You'll learn. . . . In fact, while we're here . . . would you like to learn something? Something that would make me happy? Not just me, but . . . other women?"

I thought: "What?!"

She said, "You know how you kissed me before?"

I said, "Yes!"

She said, "Well, there's another way you can kiss me."

"Oh, good!"

"Would you like to learn?"

"Yes!"

"Okay. Well, maybe we should do this gradually. Josh, why don't we start with you kissing me again on the lips."

"Okay."

"Good. Now, keep kissing me—but move down . . . slowly."

"Okay."

Hesitantly, I started moving down. Slowly.

I was under her chin.

I started to move at kind of a steady pace. I started to feel kind of like . . . a Land Rover.

Down her neck . . . between her collarbone things . . . here come her breasts . . .

I wanted to stay with her breasts! But my momentum was carrying me down to her belly button. I hovered over her belly button—and then, in a fit of inspiration, I stuck in . . . my tongue.

And I started moving my tongue around and around the rim of her belly button—one way, then the other way. I thought, "This is fun." I thought, "I'm so glad she thought of this. . . . I could do this all night. I could do this forever—I'm an oboist!" Around and around and around. . . . "I could do this over and over and over and—"

And I felt her hand on my head. Pushing me . . . down!

I came upon a ridge of hair. More hair. A whole hair region. I started kissing it. She said, "Your tongue!" I started licking it. She said, "Inside!" I went inside. She went, "Ah!" I went, "Ah!" She said, "Go back!" I went, "Ah!" She said, "No! Back where you were!"

"This *is* where I was!"

She said, "No—*exactly* where you were!"

"This *is* exactly where I was—it's inside!"

She said, "I want you to listen to me very carefully. . . . I would like you to move three millimeters up. . . . Now two and a half to the right—*your* right. . . . Now down in sort of a 45-degree arc . . ."

I felt like, you know, the pilot died, the copilot had a heart attack—*I* don't know how to fly a 747, but if I don't land the plane, everyone's gonna die!

I didn't even know what I was looking for. Maybe it was a little bump; maybe it was a bump on my tongue! And I was getting preoccupied with the taste. Salty. Not matzo, exactly, but—

She said, "There! That's it—there. Keep doing that there—until I tell you to stop."

Okay, I'm going to stay there; in fact, to anchor myself there, I'm going to hold onto her legs, which are big and cold and strong. I'm holding on; I'm going to stay there—

And she started to heave! And to undulate!

She said, "Go back there!" But the there wasn't there—it was there, it was there, it was there . . . It was a Gertrude Stein kind of conundrum: the there was not there!

I thought: "Okay—in my mind, visualize a grid. Cartesian coordinates. Okay: B-6—not there. Q-12—not there. But if we triangulate, the square of the hypotenuse is equal to the sum of—"

I went, "Ah!" She went, "Ah!" I thought, "Okay, my education is useful!"

And I was holding on there, holding on there, and Marcie's going, "Oh, Oh, Oh, Oooh, Oooooh, OOOOOOHHHHH! . . .

"Stop! . . . Stop. Stop! . . . *Very* important to stop when I say, 'Stop.' Otherwise it tickles—in a bad way. . . . Come back up here. . . . Yesh, you can . . . yesh, you can . . ."

I crawled back up and I lay down next to her, staring up at the ceiling. The paint on the ceiling was peeling: beautiful peeling Marcie peeling paint peeling.

Marcie was stroking my hair. She said, "Josh, that was very good. You're a good student. Oh, you're so young! You probably think your life is gonna be filled with exciting moments like these. And you may wonder how you'll ever fit all those exciting moments into just one life.

"But let me tell you, Josh: When you get older—when you hit . . . your twenties—you'll look ahead and you'll see your life to be one vast, flat, arid desert. And as you stumble, choking, across that desert, every once in a while you'll come upon an oasis—a tiny oasis of pleasure.

"And you'll kneel down, and you'll touch your lips to the cool damp . . . and you'll be grateful."

And one evening, a few months later—during a writers' workshop—I was in my room, filling out college applications (only to Ivy League schools, of course, because, as Grandpa pointed out when he poked his head in: "Know the enemy!"). I was still able to listen in on the workshop, because a crocheted door—while an effective-enough visual deterrent—is not so great as a sound buffer.

Especially when Sy Paskoff is reading from his latest chapter: "WHAT? What do you *WANT*?"

And I heard Grandpa leap up and go, "Whaddaya got?!"

And then, after a break, my mom started reading from the latest chapter of her teen romance. As the words came floating in, I realized that in my mom's latest chapter, her protagonist, "Josh Kornbluth," was spurning the advances of a beautiful older woman so he could remain true to his chaste young companion.

I had to get up from my bed, make my way through the kitchen . . . and look out through the kitchen doorway into the living room.

"Uh, excuse me, Mom . . . Mom? I don't think 'Josh Kornbluth' would do that."

And I looked over at Marcie, who was wearing a nice turban. And Marcie glanced up from her crocheting . . . and smiled.

When autumn came, I had made a sufficient number of visits to the Wassermanian oasis that I could go off to college and actually—Grandpa would have been proud—actually focus on my work.

But a few weeks into my second semester I got a call from Sam Vogel. Remember Sam, the big, bald . . . I guess, *pro*-Semite? He said, "Come back to New York, Josh. Your father's had a stroke."

What?!

When I got to Columbia Presbyterian, Dad was already in the ICU—the Intensive Care Unit. Right away one of the young interns came out to talk to me and Sue, my stepmother. He said, "Look, we believe in being totally honest with the family, and our honest belief is that Paul Kornbluth has had a terrible stroke. He probably will not survive. And if he does survive, he certainly will never regain consciousness."

Which hit me hard. But Sue looked right up at the young doctor and said, "That's not how *we* look at it!"

Evidently not!

So Sue and I waited outside the ICU, waiting for Dad to come out of his coma. And as we waited, we got to swap our respective theories of why Dad had had his stroke at that particular time.

To me, it seemed obvious: it was because he had just been fired from that great job. He had done really well, too. He had taken those kids—illiterate at the beginning of seventh grade—and by the end of the eighth grade, Dad and the other teachers had them reading *The Grapes of Wrath* and other cool books. And then they took another bunch of seventh-graders, and they were doing wonders with *them*. The project was a big success.

But my father wasn't the type of guy to let his success speak for itself. He'd saunter into teacher meetings and go, "My students were way behind your students, and now they're way ahead. Why?" Which endeared him to his colleagues.

And then Dad started filing grievances, against the principal, and the assistant principals, and the school board—until he got to be such a pain in the ass that they had essentially the educational equivalent of a court-martial of my father. In front of the entire school board of Stamford, Connecticut, they had a hearing to determine if my dad should be fired for—basically—insubordination.

Before the hearing we implored Dad, "Please keep your emotions in check." And he did, for a couple of hours—but then finally, after listening to all this bullshit being said about him, he just couldn't take it anymore. He stood up and essentially said to the entire school board of Stamford, Connecticut: "Fuck you!" And the entire school board of Stamford, Connecticut, essentially said to my father, "You're fired!" And a couple of weeks later, he had a stroke. To me that seemed the obvious cause-and-effect.

But Sue said, "Josh, if getting fired would cause a stroke in your father, he would have had *thousands* of strokes by now. No, Josh, I think what ultimately caused your father's stroke was his . . . drug addiction."

"What?!"

"Josh, your father was addicted to speed. Remember those little pills he used to get from that pharmacy? That was the one crooked pharmacist who would keep selling those pills to your father.

"And his doctor told him, 'Paul, you keep taking those pills, you're going to kill yourself.' But your father wouldn't listen. Till one day he decided, 'I'm going to do it. I'm going to quit.' And Josh, he did, he quit, he went cold turkey. It took two weeks; it was terrible—he had the shakes, the chills . . ."

I said, "Wait, Sue, wait. I would have noticed my dad getting the D.T.'s. I would have noticed that."

She said, "No, Josh, it's when you were in Russia. . . . And then your father decided, 'If I can quit those pills, I can do *any-thing.*' And that's when he shaved off his beard, and cut his hair, and got that great new job."

For two and a half months, Sue and I waited outside the ICU—and at the end of that time, though Dad was still in a coma, he had stabilized to the point where he could be moved into a private room. And now that he was in a private room, for the first time he could have visitors. So all the hootenanniers came in. They crammed into the tiny room. It was like a scene out of a Marx Brothers movie—although maybe a different Marx. Singing over my Dad, who's in a coma, everyone's singing:

> Arise, ye prisoner of starvation!
> Arise, ye wretched of the earth!

From far and wide, patients would wheel their things, with things stuck in their arms, they'd wheel down long corridors, just to peek in the doorway and look at this sideshow. We were like an alternative ICU: an Intensive *Communist* Unit.

One time, one of the doctors pulled me aside; he said, "You know, we all think it's very beautiful what you people are doing—but you do know, Josh, that it is quixotic, don't you?"

By this point I'd learned to just look up at him and say, "That's not how *we* look at it!"

For justice thunders condemnation!

A better world's in birth!

And after three more months, one day my dad came out of it!

His eyes opened. I was there. At first you could tell he couldn't see anything, because his eyes were just kind of wiggling around. But then as the weeks went by, he started to be able to follow my hands with his eyes; he started to move his head; he started to grunt and make sounds; he started to talk—although he had aphasia, where you can *think* of the words but you can't get them out. And then he started to move a little bit; he started to be able to feed himself. He made an incredible recovery. As it turns out, Dad did remain totally paralyzed on one side—but fortunately, we all felt, it was the politically incorrect right side.

At last Dad got to the point where he could be taken home. And I was raring to go back to college, but I felt guilty leaving Sue now to take care of Dad in his wheelchair and their three still-very-small children: Jacob, Amy, and Sammy.

But Sue said, "No, Josh, I've thought it through. Go back to college. I've decided I'm going to pack everyone else up and take them back with me to Ottawa Lake."

And that's what she did. She packed up Dad and Jacob and Amy and Sammy and took them back with her to her tiny home-town, Ottawa Lake, Michigan. And I went back to college.

And Dad started writing me letters. He'd learned how to write with his left hand.

I remember the last letter I got from him; it was written in his usual loopy, off-hand handwriting:

My son, today a garbage truck stopped in front of our house. And out of the garbage truck emerged two blond men! Where am I?

Fifty-nine years in New York, my father had never seen two blonds get out of a garbage truck. When I read that letter, I knew my dad was not in his proper milieu.

And my fears were borne out a few weeks later, when I got the call from Sue.

She said, "Josh, I'm so sorry, but your father's heart finally stopped. Please come to Ottawa Lake for the funeral."

She was right: his heart had always kept going. His brain had stopped at one point, his kidneys, his liver; but his heart had kept going. And now it had stopped.

By the time I flew in to Ottawa Lake, Sue—being so incredibly organized—had already made all the funeral arrangements. In fact, to appease my father's parents, whom he loathed, and who loathed him . . . but to appease them, Sue had arranged for a traditional Jewish ceremony. She'd even found a rabbi to come in to Ottawa Lake!

So we all crowded into the little Catholic chapel in town: the forty-five or so Ottawa Lakeans, and the family, of course, and the hootenanniers, who had flown in from New York.

The rabbi went up into the pulpit—and the rabbi . . . I mean, she was nice, she seemed bright, but she hadn't known my dad. So the rabbi gave this kind of generic eulogy:

"Paul Kornbluth, by all accounts, was a fine, responsible father." I'm sitting in the back of the chapel thinking, *Well, he did leave me and my mom when I was six months old because his therapist told him to....*

"Paul Kornbluth, by all accounts, was a fine, responsible teacher." I'm thinking: *"Fuck you!" "You're fired!"*

"Paul Kornbluth, by all accounts, was an American who truly loved his country." I'm thinking: *Well ... in his own way ...*

I was willing to grin and bear it; it's just a stupid ceremony. But sitting next to me was the Reverend Chuck Yerkes. He's used to *running* these sorts of events. And he was squirming in his seat; I could tell he couldn't stand hearing his best friend described in these generic terms.

Sure enough, in the middle of the rabbi's eulogy, Chuck just couldn't take it anymore. He stood up in the back of the chapel and said, "Excuse me! May I give an alternative eulogy?"

And the rabbi said, "Okay," and sat down. (I guess they have that arrangement among religious people—that if one person asks, the first one takes the bench and the other one goes up to the front.)

And Chuck went up into the pulpit and gave his eulogy for my dad:

"It's true, what the good rabbi said—to a point. Paul Kornbluth *was* a fine, loving father—and a passionate, dedicated teacher. But it should also be said that Paul Kornbluth was ... a

Marxist-Leninist. He believed in the violent destruction of this nation's government. Heads will roll in Washington because of this man! Blood will flow through the streets! And not just in Washington. Here in Ottawa Lake, the fascists will be *crushed*—their skulls carried on sticks through the town!"

Everyone in the chapel is going, "AAAAAH!" Even us in the family: "AAAAAH!"

I was still shaking as we made our way to the cemetery for the actual burial. The rabbi handed each of us the shovel: me, Sue, Jacob, Amy, and Sammy. And we each put a shovelful of dirt onto the lid of Dad's coffin in the hole. Then the rabbi handed us mimeographed sheets of the Kaddish, the Jewish prayer for the dead. And we said the Kaddish, and then they covered my father up.

And I went walking on the path leading out of the cemetery ahead of everyone else. I guess I wanted to get my head together.

And there must have been a slight downhill grade to the path—because without even thinking about it, I just started singing:

> As I go down in the valley to pray
> Studying about that good old way
> And who shall wear the robe and crown
> Good Lord, show me the way.

And my oldest little sibling, Jacob, who was about six at the time . . . I guess he heard me—because he came running up to walk alongside me and sing along:

> Oh, brothers, let's go down
> Let's go down, won't you come on down
> Come on, brothers, let's go down
> Down to the valley to pray.

We kept walking. And the road flattened out—as they'll do out there in the Midwest. So we started singing "flat" songs—rounds:

> Come follow, follow, follow, follow, follow, follow me.
> Whither shall I follow, follow, follow
> Whither shall I follow, follow thee?

> Whither shall I follow, follow, follow
> Whither shall I follow, follow thee?

the

mathematics

of change

Let's start with functions, why don't we?

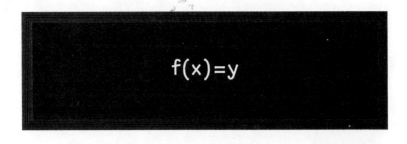

$$f(x) = y$$

A function is a transformative experience. It's kind of like a machine—you go into the function machine and you get . . . changed. Well, *you* don't go into the machine—usually *x* goes into the machine. Mathematicians describe this situation as "*f of x.*" *x* goes into *f*, the function machine, and it gets transformed into . . . *y*. No one knows the reason for this—why *x* almost always gets transformed into *y*. But let's just accept it for now.

And *x* is the kind of thing you'd *want* to put inside a transformative machine, because *x* is a *variable*. You wouldn't want to put, say, *c* inside the machine, because *c* is a *constant*. And a constant is . . . constant. You go up to a constant: "How're ya doing today, constant?" "Fine." Next day: "How're ya doing?" "Fine." Next day: "Fine." It's a constant!

But a variable: "Well, how're ya doing today, variable?" "Oh, pretty good." Next day: "Great!" Next day: "Lousy!" You know, it's a variable!

And mathematicians have focused on what happens to *x* when it's inside the machine, and what happens after it emerges. Less attention, I think, has been paid to that moment just before *x* enters the function machine. As it stands there, at the threshold of some new experience, not knowing what's about to befall it. Standing there—trembling, tremulous . . .

Standing, or sometimes . . . *sitting*—sitting in folding chairs arrayed neatly all along the great North Lawn of the Princeton University campus.

We were the incoming freshmen of Princeton, and this was our first day at college. They had announced over the loud-speaker: "Incoming freshmen!" We all *ducked*.

Sitting in our folding chairs. Facing us was the big main administrative building: Nassau Hall (because Princeton used to be just Nassau College).

Also facing us, in front of Nassau Hall, was the president of Princeton, President Bowen. Not, uh, a real . . . *ethnic*-looking guy—but *focused*.

He, in turn, was flanked by two stone tigers. Tigers being the mascot of Princeton—representing, as they do, the ancient ferocity of the WASP peoples.

Up behind President Bowen were the elder statesmen among the Board of Alumni—old gents with their canes, pointing them up at the sky: "We *own* those clouds! We *own* those trees! Ha ha ha ha ha!"

President Bowen said, "Welcome. Welcome, class of 1980. You know, each incoming class is unique. In fact, this uniqueness is what each incoming class . . . shares. Can any among you tell me what is unique about 1980?"

Well, to me it was obvious right away: I mean, *1980* was divisible by *4!*

$$1+9+8+0=18$$

It's a trick, you see. If you take any number, and the last two digits are divisible by *4*, then the *entire* number is divisible by *4*.

80 can be divided by *4*, therefore *1980* is divisible by *4*—so *1980* can be divided by *4*, which of course is *2* times *2*.

Now, another trick: if you add any number across—in this case, *1* plus *9* is *10* . . . plus *8* is *18*. If you add all the numbers across and that sum is divisible by *3*, that means the *entire* number is divisible by *3*. Since *18* is divisible by *3*, that means *1980* is divisible by *3*.

And if the number is *even* and the sum is divisible by *3*, that means the *entire* number is divisible by *6*. (Of course, we could have known that already, because we knew we already had *2* times *3*.)

Now, since our number ends in *0*, that means, of course, that it's divisible by *10*—which means it's divisible by *2* times *5*. In fact, *1980* is *10* times *198*, *198* being a multiple of *11* . . .

These are the kinds of tricks my dad taught me.

He would pick me up from my mom's and take me the six or seven blocks to the 168th Street station of the subway. We'd go down and down into the incredibly fetid air of that subway station. We'd get onto the Broadway Local. And we'd sit down on

1

seats that were woven and cushiony in those days, not plastic the way they are now. We'd sit down in our seats and right away Dad would turn to me and say: "Your mother is a very crazy woman." I'd go: "I know." So we'd get that out of the way.

And now we could move on to math. Math being one of my father's twin passions, the other one being Communism. My dad, a lifelong Communist, also a lifelong lover of mathematics. In fact, he was a math teacher—in grade school, in middle school, and often in Special Ed.

And all around us on the subway, people would be bopping each other, being bopped, mugging each other, getting mugged, spraying things on the inside, on the outside of the train, hanging off of things, hanging out of things and into things . . . But we were in our own world—our world of math. And dad would take out his little index cards and show me tricks . . .

He started by teaching me the numerals. The first numeral I can remember learning was . . . 1.

1: tall, fragile, delicate . . . very much like my mom. And my mom had recently slipped on a patch of ice and bruised her knees, and for some reason this affected me very deeply. So from that time on, I always made sure to give my 1's those little feet, for

support. And I'd give them a little cap, you know, just for style. *1:* very fragile.

Not like *3,* with its beautiful, nurturing curves—I *like 3!* But then, one day I happened to be approaching my beloved *3* from the wrong direction and . . . *ow!* It *pierced* me! That's when I learned about the terrible schizophrenia that numbers can have. They can help you, they can hurt you—it all depends from which side you approach them. *3:* very unpredictable, very scary.

Not like *6. 6,* shaped very much like my dad, with his nice potbelly. *6,* which would then spin round and round and round and would end up as . . . *9.*

9, the most beautiful and mystically powerful of all the numerals. *9,* with its huge brain staring down beneficently on all the smaller numerals. *9,* so mystical, so powerful . . .

For example: *9,* though it was of course the largest numeral, could, in an instant, turn itself into *0.* This was part of a trick called "Casting Out Nines" that my dad showed me on the train one day. He said, "My son, let's pick two numbers at random. How about . . . *1848* and *1917?* Just *any* two numbers at random.

$$1848 = 21 = 3$$
$$\underline{1917} = 18 = \cancel{9}$$
$$3765 = 21 = ⓷$$

"Now, first, let's add them together: *1848* plus *1917* equals *3765*. Now, we check our calculations by Casting Out Nines. . . ."

What Casting Out Nines involves is that you add across and you *keep* adding across until you have a single-digit numeral. And then you add down and you check. And if at any point you get a *9*, then you can turn it into a *0*—that's why it's called "Casting Out Nines"!

Well, let's do it.

1 plus *8* is *9*, *9* plus *4* is *13*, *13* plus *8* is *21*—and now we've run into a single-digit number, so we keep adding. We add the *2* and the *1* and we get *3*.

Okay, now on the second line, *1917*, we have *1* plus *9* is *10*, *10* plus *1* is *11*, *11* plus *7* is *18*, *1* plus *8* adds up to *9*. Let's "cast out" that *9*, so we get *0*.

And now we add down: *3* plus *0* adds up to *3*. Now we check. In the sum, *3* plus *7* is *10*, *10* plus *6* is *16*, *16* plus *5* is *21*, *2* plus *1* adds up to . . . *3!*

Of course, it could have been done a lot more slickly—a lot more *efficiently*—if I had cast out my nines at the earliest opportunity. For instance, going back to *1848* here, *8* plus *1* adds up to

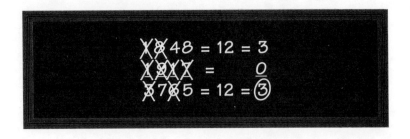

$$X\!\!\!\!/\,8\!\!\!\!/\,48 = 12 = 3$$
$$X\!\!\!\!/\,X\!\!\!\!/\,X\!\!\!\!/ =\quad\underline{0}$$
$$8\!\!\!\!/\,7\!\!\!\!/\,6\!\!\!\!/\,5 = 12 = ③$$

9, so we could just cast it out right off the get-go. Then we just add the 4 and the 8 that remain—which adds up to 12, which gets us back to 3. Now on the second line we cast out the 9—and 7 plus 1 plus 1 also adds up to 9, so we can cast out this *entire number* and turn it into 0. Now, in the sum, let's cast out 3 plus 6, which adds up to 9; so we just have 7 plus 5, which adds up to 12, which gets us back to . . . 3!

Mystical . . . Powerful . . . It was armed with the power of 9 that I was able to blow away my competition . . . in second-grade math class.

Our teacher, Mr. Cavanaugh, was a small, compact, very intense guy. Always seemed to be about to blow some very big gasket, Mr. Cavanaugh. (Also, I think, a very *patriotic* guy.) And whenever he got the sense that people weren't paying the proper amount of attention, he would *slam* the blackboard with his fist: "DAMMIT!" And when he slammed the blackboard particularly hard, a lot of the pieces of chalk would fall off the bottom ledge onto the floor and they would shatter. And then he'd pick up the little half-pieces of chalk and hold them in his middle fingers, and he'd go:

"PAY ATTENTION! PAY . . . ATTENTION! . . . Okay, let's

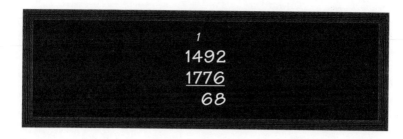

1
1492
<u>1776</u>
68

do some addition. Let's take two numbers at random. How about
. . . *1492* and *1776*. Just any two numbers at random. Now,
who would like to add these two numbers together? I know *you*
would, Mr. Kornbluth. Anyone else? How about *you*, Mr.
Warren?"

Oh, I loved it when he called on Ruben Warren! Ruben Warren was my tormentor in second grade. He was the big bully in
our class. Ruben Warren was always picking on me because I
was a little chubby and had kind of a big head and was really
good at math. Ruben Warren was the master of his domain,
which was the schoolyard. So I loved to see it when he had to go
up to *my* turf: the blackboard.

Ruben got up. Had to release the wrist of the kid sitting next to
him. Walked up to the blackboard, with his little red Prince
Valiant haircut . . .

"Okay, um, *2* plus *6* is, uh . . . *8*—right. (Thanks, Billy—you'll
live.) Now, uh, *9* plus *7* is, um . . . (Billy?!) Okay, put the *6* down
here, carry the *1* . . ."

Mr. Cavanaugh leapt up. "NO, Mr. Warren! You don't WRITE
OUT the number that you carry. That's *weak!* WEAK! Hold it in
your mind, Mr. Warren. HOLD IT IN YOUR MIND! Mr.

$$14 \cancel{9} 2 = \qquad 7$$
$$\underline{1776} = 21 = \underline{3}$$
$$\cancel{3}2\cancel{6}8 = 10 = 1$$

Warren, what do you plan to be when you grow up—besides incarcerated, that is?"

"I dunno, maybe a astronaut?"

"Well, Mr. Warren, then let's say, God forbid, NASA hires you. They go, 'Excuse me, Mr. Warren, but how far away is Sputnik?' Instead of saying, '*1492*,' you go, 'It's eleven thousand four hundred ninety-two.' You see? You made a mistake because you wrote out the number that you carried. That's *weak*—WEAK! HOLD IT IN YOUR MIND! . . .

"And what are *you* chortling about, Mr. Kornbluth?"

I said, "Well sir, I long ago did that simple addition—and since then I've also checked my addition using a simple trick my dad taught me called Casting Out Nines."

"Would you care to share this trick with the rest of us, Mr. Kornbluth?"

"Certainly, sir."

So I went up to the blackboard (covertly giving Ruben the finger).

"Okay, so here's how I did it. On the first line I cast out this *9* right here. And add across: *1* plus *4* is *5, 5* plus *2* is *7.* Now, on the second line, *1* plus *7* is *8, 8* plus *7* is *15, 15* plus *6* is *21,* which I then add up to get . . . 3. Now I add the 7 and the 3 to-gether to get 10, which adds up to 1. Okay, now on the bottom we cast out this 6 and 3, which add up to 9, so we have 8 and 2, which add up to 10—which gets us back to 1!"

"Mr. Kornbluth, you seem pretty smug. Are you aware, though, that this little trick your father taught you—this Casting Out Nines—are you aware that this does not in fact *prove* that your addition was correct?"

"Uh . . . no?"

"No, Mr. Kornbluth. All it proves is that your addition *could* have been correct. . . . Ahh, so *now* we see that smile start to fade. Oh, Mr. Kornbluth, what I'd give to be there that one fine day when you finally . . . *hit the wall.*"

Hit the wall?

"Dad, what's 'hitting the wall'? Dad, why doesn't Casting Out Nines work? Dad, Mr. Cavanaugh said . . ."

But my father didn't hear me—because we were moving, moving again. Dad didn't hear me, because while he was carry-ing the big bookcase down the stairs—from the sixth floor down to the first floor—he was repeating his moving mantra over and over: "It's not that it's heavy, it's that it's bulky. It's not that it's heavy, it's that it's bulky. . . ."

It's like going up to Atlas and saying, "Excuse me, Mr. Atlas, how's the world doing?"

"It's not that it's heavy, it's that it's bulky."

The idea being that no real man should have any trouble with anything heavy, but *bulk*—no one could deal with *bulk*. "It's not that it's heavy, it's that it's bulky."

My father, as I've said, a Communist, a man not given to those little intermediary steps. While a lot of his friends from City College when he was an undergraduate had taken these little tiny steps towards some sort of success, Dad was waiting to take that *one big leap*—that leap that he would take, that the people of America and the world would take, towards happiness and Communism and freedom. My dad, not given to those little intermediary steps. For example: he's carrying down the bookcase—he hasn't taken out the books.

"It's not that it's heavy, it's that it's bulky. It's not that it's heavy, it's that it's bulky. . . ."

"Dad, what's 'hitting the wall'?"

"It's not that it's heavy, it's that it's bulky."

And Dad hit the lobby and tripped on a loose tile and almost slammed his head into the bookcase. "Oy! . . . What's that, my son? You're asking about 'hitting the wall'? It's a term for something that happens to *some* people in math. It'll never happen to you. . . . Why? I'll tell you— No, I'll *show* you."

And he started *running* back up the stairs. I followed him—up and up, *past* the sixth floor, up through the big metal door I'd never been through, up onto the roof. And Dad took me all the way out . . . to the edge.

"My son, do you recognize what you see before you?"

"Of course, Dad. That's the George Washington Bridge. It's

only a few blocks away. It's the one thing that connects me with Palisades Amusement Park."

"My son, what would you say if I told you that one day you will possess that bridge?"

"You mean, like, the way all people will one day possess all things? Or, uh, . . . me *personally?*"

"I mean you, personally, my son. You'll possess that bridge by holding it . . . in your mind. And your tool to do that will be . . . *math.*

"My son, look at those mighty cables holding up the bridge—straight lines! You'll possess those through . . . *geometry.* Look at those pebbles strewn along the bottom of the bridge—you'll possess those, as abstractions, through . . . *algebra.* And my son, those curves, those mighty curves that hold up the bridge—to possess those you'll need . . . *calculus*—the mathematics of change.

"Oh, my son, I loved calculus so much back when I took it at City College—until one day when I . . . I hit the wall.

"But you won't hit the wall. No, my son. You will burst through every wall that has hitherto existed. You will go on to become THE GREATEST MATHEMATICIAN WHO HAS EVER LIVED!"

Wow!

At the age of nine, all of a sudden I have a purpose—nay, a *destiny.* I'm going to become . . . the greatest mathematician who ever lived. And it's all going to start with *calculus*—and I can't wait to get there.

But in order to get there, I have to go through all this *baby math stuff!*

Which is what I did. I went through, you know, addition, subtraction, multiplication, division . . . Then I went on to the Bronx High School of Science, where the first year we learned all about . . . *geometry.* In geometry we learned from the ancient Egyptians—indirectly—that you need not traverse your land to know the area of it. No. All you need to traverse is just two of the sides, and you multiply those sides together and you get the area.

I thought this was very beautiful, very elegant. Others in my class did not find it so. Others hit the wall in geometry. Fortunately, it wasn't too late to transfer back to Performing Arts.

The next year we learned all about . . . *algebra.* In algebra we learned from the ancient Greeks—again, indirectly—that you need not traverse *any* of your land to get the area. You can just sit in your sandbox all day and work things out with a stick, using abstractions like *x, y,* and *z* . . . I mean, sure, every once in a while you might get attacked by a Roman soldier with a knife, but basically I loved it. Others, however, they hit the wall at algebra.

But this was nothing compared to the carnage at *trig.* Trigonometry, the mathematics of triangles. Oh my God, everything turns

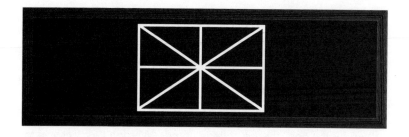

into a triangle, everything. Take this rectangle—that's *two* triangles, no, it's *four*, no, it's *eight!* . . . It's *lots and lots* of triangles!

All around me, kids were impaling themselves on triangles. Some were going inside triangles, *never to emerge.*

I, however, loved trig—especially seeing as now I was just one year away from calculus, the mathematics of change. But I didn't want to take little kiddie calculus—you know, the A.P. class you can take senior year in high school. I wanted to take real, grown-up, adult calculus—the kind you can take in college. So I applied for early admission to Princeton, with its famous math department. And I got my application, and it had this part to fill in where you were supposed to say, essentially, what you wanted to be when you grew up. Well, all *I* wanted to do was do math. *That's all I wanted to do.* But there was this great big space to fill in—so I wrote,

I WANT TO DO MATH!

And evidently they saw the fervor of my conviction, and I was accepted.

So there I was, trembling in my folding chair among all the other tremulous variables. Madly in my head, I'm factoring out *1980*, when I realize that President Bowen has moved on to another topic! Evidently that question had been . . . rhetorical.

"In closing, I would just like to explain what we expect of all of you by the end of your college career. We don't expect you to have become *scholars*. No. All we expect you to become is . . . *alumni*. Wealthy, generous alumni. We've been trying to come up with a way of turning you into alumni without having to put up with you for four years—but having failed at that, all we ask is that you get through your undergraduate years as quickly and efficiently as possible. And now, all of ye—disperse to thy respective areas of concentration."

So we all dispersed to our prospective majors. This was in 1976, which I like to think of as kind of the tail end of the Sixties. I mean, if you sort of imagine a *long* tail, like an iguana tail, at the tip of the tail there were just these little glimmers left of Sixties idealism. But mostly, at this point it was the pre-Eighties. Everything was "pre-"—pre-law, pre-med, pre-business, pre-death . . . everything was "pre-."

And everyone went off to their little areas of interest. The pre-business majors went off to construct their little bagel wagons; the pre-law students went off to their fencing lessons; the pre-English majors went to their simulation seminars on how to drive a cab . . .

But for those of us who were pre-Einsteins, it was easy to find *our* destination: the math building was the tallest building on campus. There it was—Fine Hall—rising up way above everything else. And Fine Hall was a relatively recent addition to the campus. Most of the buildings were old, and covered with ivy, and had gargoyles on top—although often the gargoyles turned out to be alumni.

Like most of the buildings on campus, Fine Hall had been built with funds donated by a wealthy alumnus—in this case, a Mr. Fine, who'd specified that Fine Hall, if he donated the money for it, had to be the tallest building on campus. This wasn't unusual. Wealthy alumni would go to President Bowen all the time; they'd go, "President Bowen, I'll give you the money for the building, but it must be shaped like my sister." Or, "I'll give you the money for the building, but it must act like a giant Crockpot."

And Mr. Fine had evidently gone, "Well, President Bowen, I'll give you the money to build the math building, but it has to be the tallest building on campus." And President Bowen had gone, "Well, you know, Mr. Fine, by ancient rules here at Princeton, the tallest point on campus is supposed to be the very tip of the steeple of the chapel—sort of out of deference to . . . God."

"Well, okay, just no check-y."

"Uh . . . never mind. (Sorry, God.) Thanks, Mr. Fine."

As I approached Fine Hall, I could see the other math freshmen converging. We were all recognizable by the glint coming off of our pocket protectors.

In order to get into the building, we had to go around one of the many original sculptures that dot the Princeton campus. This particular sculpture was by Alexander Calder, and it was made of black metal, with lots of points. And you know, I had seen a lot of Calder's stuff on field trips when I was a kid in New York; many were very lovely—wistful, whimsical clowns, circuses. This was not one of those. Calder had made this sculpture on a bad day. His girlfriend had gone, "Sandy Calder, you're a lousy lay, and I don't like you."

"Grrr—I'm gonna build a sculpture, and I'm gonna make it *pointy,* with lots of *points,* big POINTS, and big black rivets, like the rivets she stuck into my soul!"

And some alum had *bought* it, and had donated it to Princeton. And he'd gone, "President Bowen, I bought you this Calder statue."

"Oh, is it one of those whimsical—"

"Well, you've got to *see* it, really."

In the lobby of Fine Hall we were greeted by the guard. We all gave one another a kind of look, as if to go, "Why does the math building *need* a guard?"

But it turns out he was a burnt-out grad student—and this was one of the ways they recycled them. Many of them had been there so long, they'd forgotten how to *leave*. The ones who'd been there the very longest were just now on that toggle point between mass and energy. Like, you'd see one on a path and you'd wave to him, and you'd realize you'd just walked *through* him somehow.

The guard said, "Welcome! Welcome to what I like to call the Ivory Tower. I myself used to be one of you, and now, well, *look.*

. . . Ah, never mind. . . . Well, we *could* start here at the bottom, but why not start at the top? Hey!"

So we got on the elevator with the slightly weird guard. And as we went up through the lower floors, we could feel that the air was kind of close, kind of swamplike—and we knew we were in the realm of *applied math*. Then, as we went up higher and higher, the air got more and more rarefied, and our ears started popping—and we knew we were entering the realm of *pure math*.

Finally we reached the very top floor, and the elevator doors opened—BING!—onto the very top of pure math.

"Yup!" the guard said. "You can feel it in the air, can't you? Some of the most brilliant mathematicians on earth have their offices right here on this floor. For example, in this office we have Professor Phil Crowder—known, of course, for his famous 'Crowder Theorem' . . . which we're *sure* he's just about to prove. Crowder has posited that a number does exist between *8* . . . and itself. Not as simple as it sounds!

"Technically, yes, Crowder will be your professor in Math 101, in calculus. You'll never meet him.

"You'll notice, all along the hallways, these blackboards. That's so a brilliant mathematician like Crowder, if he's on his way to the bathroom, and he suddenly gets an idea, he can disgorge himself *intellectually,* if you will, before disgorging himself *physically*—which is essential, apparently."

As the other freshmen went to disgorge themselves on the blackboard, I doubled back, because I had noticed that Crow-

der's door seemed to be just slightly ajar. I looked in through the crack of the doorway—and *there he was,* the great man himself! He was at the blackboard, and he was having . . . a *moment.*

He was tall. Tall and thin. And he had these patches of hair on the top of his head that went straight up—because he was thinking *so hard,* and he was so close . . . to God!

I moved on. But in that moment, I'd had confirmed for me the fondest of my hopes and expectations: my hope that way up here, at these very highest reaches of pure math, there were things to be experienced that could be experienced nowhere else. And I meant to experience them!

When I rejoined the group, everyone was questioning the guard closely as to why we couldn't go up onto the roof.

He said, "Well, the door's locked."

We said, "Why is that?"

"Well, it's the highest point on campus."

"What does *that* have to do with anything?"

"Okay, uh . . . Sometimes a student will, you know, feel the pressure—and will want to go up *through* that door, up onto the roof . . . and then will, like, *defenestrate*—often onto the, um, Calder."

$$0.9999999 \ldots = 1$$

"My god! Well, *we're* not gonna feel that kind of pressure. Why? 'Cause we're fucking *brilliant,* that's why! . . . In fact, when do we get going? *When do we show our stuff?"*

So there I was—back on the very first floor of Fine Hall, in the very front row of a packed lecture hall. Waiting for our first calculus class, our first Math 101 lecture, to begin. "I wanna get going—I wanna show my stuff!"

After what seemed like an eternity, in came our grad student T.A.

"Welcome. Welcome to Math 101, the very bottom of the mathematical curriculum. Some of you may find that this course goes too quickly for you to follow it. This will not mean you're not smart. It *will* mean you're not smart *enough.* Not to worry, though—there's always stuff you can do . . . with your hands.

"*Limits!*

"What I'm about to write down on the blackboard should be, to all of you, both trivial and obvious: *0.999 . . .* on and on and on into infinity equals *1.* An example of an infinite series converging on a *limit* of . . . 1. Got it? Good.

"Now, let's take a function. Start with something *simple,* like

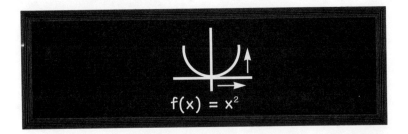

$f(x)$ equals x^2. As x approaches 2, y approaches 4. x approaches 2 . . . limit. y approaches 4 . . . limit. Limit, limit, limit. Limit, limit, limit, limit, limit. . . . It's that simple."

As everyone streamed out of the lecture hall, they looked as if they knew exactly what the T.A. had been talking about. I, however—I had some questions. I mean, I *kind* of got how *0.999 . . .* could approach *1*. I mean, here's *0*, here's *1*. Now, *0.9* would be close to *1*. *0.99* would be even closer to *1*. *0.999* would be even closer. *0.9999*, even closer. . . . So I could see it getting closer and closer to *1*. I mean, very, very close to *1*. Just awfully close. I just didn't see where it actually . . . *became 1*.

Maybe I should get the textbook.

In fact, that's just one of several hurdles we freshmen have to leap in order to get where we're going. I have to buy my textbook . . . get myself a job . . . and take the swimming test.

I decided to put these tasks in some kind of rational order. I decided first I would get myself a job, which would *make* me money. Then I would buy my textbooks, which would *cost* me money. And then I would take the swimming test, which would likely cost me my life.

In order to get a job, I had to go into Nassau Hall itself. As I made my way through this huge main administrative building, I realized right away that virtually everyone in this building was devoting virtually all their time to raising money from wealthy alumni.

Passing open doorways, I'd hear one side of people's telephone conversations: "Look, sir, your class is way behind all the other classes—we have information on you, sir, we have we have pictures. . . ."

Past another doorway: "Yes, sir, we're very optimistic about those implants. We're going to put a few in some freshmen as they sleep, and if they work out, we'll never have to rely on their families to track them down, ever again. . . ."

Then on up to the third floor, where I went past the office of President Bowen himself: "Look, Herb. What part of you do you want me to kiss? I'm *not* being euphemistic. . . ."

Finally I entered the office of the one administrator who was actually known for dealing with student-related issues: Dean Pablo Lucci, a very friendly and effusive guy. "Ah, come right in, Josh! Come in! Josh Kornbluth, is it? Sit down. No, you don't have to say a word: I already know everything about you. In fact, Josh, I chose your application as my favorite from your entire incoming class. I keep it right here in my drawer. You WANT TO DO MATH! And I think that's great. Now what can I do for you?"

"Well, Dean Lucci, I'd like to get a job. Preferably in . . . math."

"I'm sorry, Josh, there are no positions that we have for

research assistants in math. I mean, what would you do—*multiply* for them? . . . But I do see *one* job-opening in the sciences. It's in . . . biology."

"Biology? No, sir, not biology—not yucky, gunky biology. You know, where you open up the frogs and they smell like formaldehyde, or rotten eggs . . . no no no, I can't, I can't, I can't."

"Well okay, Josh, we still have plenty of jobs open in Food Services—"

"Okay, biology. Fine."

So I went to check in for my job in biology. I entered the old biology building, made my way through the dimly lit atrium, past skeletons of what *looked* like freshmen but I'm sure were something else. . . . I found my boss, Professor Schmertz—a great big man, in front of a great big lecture hall, apparently preparing to give a very big lecture.

"Ah, come in! You're my new freshman. Josh, is it? Welcome, welcome!

"Josh, as you can see, I'm kind of busy right now—preparing to deliver a very major lecture to my colleagues—but let me just very quickly explain to you what your duties for me shall entail: essentially, Josh, what I'd like you to do is give very bad diseases to mice. Cancer, usually. In fact, we have a syringe of cancer right here!

"Now, Josh, imagine you had a mouse here—I wish I could show you, but I'm very busy just now . . . Imagine you had a mouse. What you want to do is squirt a little bit of cancer under the skin here, then take the next mouse, and so on and so on.

Josh, I really wish I could show you, but I'm very busy now. I'm sure you'll do *just fine.*"

I made my way down the hallway, with my syringe of . . . *cancer!* I found out where the animal rooms were: not here on the first floor. Not in the basement. Not even in the second sub-basement. They were down in the third, and bottom, sub-basement.

So I went down and down in the elevator, and it opened up—BING!—onto . . . the smell of smells. The smell of every one of God's creatures—every cricket, every aardvark—having done every possible activity . . . and all these activities imprinted on this . . . *smell.* As I made my way down the hallway, in search of the mouse room, occasionally I would see a stray bunny rabbit hopping down the corridor. I thought, "Who's in charge here?!"

Finally I found the mouse room. As I opened the door, I could hear all the mice inside happily chirping to each other. As soon as they saw me—*silence.*

"You're the new freshman, aren't you?"

"Uh, yeah."

"You're going to give us cancer, aren't you?"

"Uh . . . no. Cancer? Ha ha. No."

"Well, then, why the big 'C' on the syringe?"

"Oh, uh . . . you mean, you've never heard of Linus Pauling? Believe me, you'll never catch cold again! In fact, why don't I start with *you,* Mr. Talkative-Mouse-Guy? . . . Okay, now don't wriggle, don't wriggle. Just stop wriggling! I'm just going to inject you with a little— JUST HOLD STILL. . . .

"Now, why'd you do that? Why'd you run away like that? . . .

"OW! . . . Have I just injected myself with . . . *cancer?!* On my very first day of college?! . . . And if I *have*, what's the gestation period for this thing? Will I have it four years, get a degree, and then *plotz?*"

I ran down the hallway, back up the elevator, down the main-floor corridor, and burst into the huge lecture hall.

"Excuse me, ladies and gentlemen! I'm sorry to interrupt this august gathering. It's just that I have to have a word with Professor Schmertz here. . . . Hello, Professor—remember me? I'm Josh, the freshman you just hired? Well, guess what? Thanks to you, I JUST INJECTED MYSELF WITH CANCER!"

"Put me down, young man! (All of you just talk amongst yourselves—just a little misunderstanding here.) Okay, now tell me, young man: you injected yourself with the syringe I gave you?"

"Oh, no, not the syringe you gave me—a syringe I brought with me from home—I filled it with Tang— YES, THE SYRINGE YOU GAVE ME!"

"Calm down, young man. You have nothing to worry about, because the syringe *I* gave you was filled with *mouse* cancer."

"*Mouse* cancer? What does that mean? I'm going to grow a long nose and a tail, and *then* plotz?"

"No, ha ha—it means that nothing whatsoever will happen to you. Mouse cancer can only affect *mice*. . . . You don't believe me? Here, give me that syringe. Look, I'm injecting myself with mouse cancer. See? Now what do you think is going to happen to me? I'm going to go home, try to hug my lovely wife—but no, I can't, 'cause I've got a big tumor? Look, I'm injecting my leg, now my other leg. You think I'll be able to jump really high? No! Look—I'm injecting my colleagues. See, they love it! (Now, wait your turn, everyone! There's plenty of mouse cancer to go around.) See, young man? Totally harmless. Young man? Young man? . . . Where'd he go?"

"Excuse me, Dean Lucci, I'm sorry to come bursting back into your office like this. I know it's only been about a half-hour since I was last here. I just don't think that biology job is going to work out for me. . . . Well, I've already had a little mishap: I just, uh, injected myself with *cancer.* . . . Oh, not to worry, it's just mouse cancer—it can't affect me. . . . Uh, do you need that cheese? . . . Anyhow, I was just wondering if you had *any* other openings—"

"As a matter of fact, Josh, another job *has* opened up in the sciences—it's in physics."

"Physics? Aw, jeez . . . all right."

Physics had always been my fallback, in case I should somehow hit my head, get brain damage, and not be able to do math. I could then do physics.

The physics building was easy to find, because it was right across the plaza from Fine Hall. But whereas the math building had to be the tallest building on campus, the wealthy alum who had donated the money for the physics building had attached a quite different requirement:

"President Bowen, I want you to make the physics building the squattest building on campus! You hear me? The absolutely squattest, squattest building on campus!"

"Yes, sir, Mr. Quasimodo, Class of '01—"

"The squattest building! . . . And ring the bell—BONG!—ring the bell—BONG!!"

I asked the receptionist where my job might be. She said, "Down at the cyclotron."

I said, "Uh, . . . down? Would that be in the . . . first sub-basement?"

"No."

"Um . . . the second sub-basement?"

"No."

Of course! It's in the third, and bottom, sub-basement. "And that would be because . . . ?" Sure—it's *radioactive.*

Down and down in the elevator, till—BING!—the elevator doors opened onto this huge, whirring metal egg: the cyclotron. Evidently spinning around within itself these little, tiny subatomic particles.

The cyclotron was being operated by these two guys: Irv and Marv. Irv seemed always to be turning the cyclotron *up—whir—* Marv seemed always to be turning it *down—whir.* There seemed to be some sort of competition between them. Up—*whir—* down—*whir—*up—*whir—*down—*whir.* And they both had this kind of hunched-over aspect that the experimental physicists down at the cyclotron tended to have, because they knew that everyone else looked down on them.

I mean, going back up to the top of Fine Hall, the pure mathematicians—like Crowder—if they would deign to look down on anybody, they'd probably look no further than the applied mathematicians on the floors below them. Because *those* guys actually had to *write things down.*

Then the applied mathematicians—if *they* looked down on anybody—they'd probably look down on the pure physics people, at the very top of the physics building, because they actually had to deal with the physical universe.

And then the pure physicists, they—and everyone else—looked down on the *applied* physicists: the guys at the cyclotron. Because those guys *actually turned knobs!* They had Ph.D.'s in physics, and they turned knobs.

And they *counted* things!

"How many neutrinos did you see, Irv?"

"I saw eleven."

"Jeez, I saw twelve—but they're so *little!*"

Then they saw me standing there in the doorway, and they came up and gave me this curious greeting, by feeling my arms. Then they gave each other a little look, as if to say, "He'll do."

"Come here—Josh, is it? Come here, Josh. . . . Okay, so here's what your duties for us basically will entail.

"We've got a loose bolt that's, um, *inside* the cyclotron. What we'd like you to do is, take this wrench—*with your hand*—and put the wrench, um, *inside* the cyclotron, and hold that loose bolt. And we'll tighten it from the *outside.* Got that? Hold the bolt *inside* the cyclotron, and we'll tighten it from the *outside.* Okay?"

I took the wrench and said, "Okay, guys, I'll do it. Of course, I'm just a novice here. You wouldn't have to turn the machine *off* first or anything, would you?"

"Oh, no, Josh. No. You take in a lot of calcium, don't you? You'll be fine."

So I put my arm, with the wrench, inside the cyclotron. And as I held the loose bolt, I could feel—*whir*—*whir*—the sensation of what I *imagined* was the feeling of quarks whizzing through my forearm. My arm felt like it was *swelling* a bit.

I said, "Hey, guys. I think maybe I'm just destined for Food Services."

They said, "Well okay, Josh, you can pass up this job—but if you do, you won't get your own . . . *office.*"

My own office!

Gray cinder block. Green, gunmetal desk. Chair that leans back. . . . Oh, it's beautiful!

"Yes, Josh—and you can spend all the time you want here. You can *live* here if you'd like. All we ask is that you occasionally help us out with the cyclotron. *And,* of course, keep an eye on Enrico."

Enrico was the mascot of the Cyclotron Group. Enrico was a large, albino catfish. And not, I would venture to say, attractive— even by *fish* standards. He was white and puffy—and slightly, uh, luminescent. And he had these little red walleyes, and this protruding lower jaw. He was constantly scraping along the bottom of the tank. And he had these whiskers that hung down from his

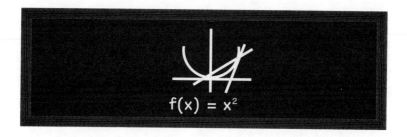

$$f(x) = x^2$$

chin, and seemed to be probing the bottom of the tank for his own fecal matter . . . and then gently lifting it up to his lips.

Watch Enrico? Help out at the cyclotron? And in return for those two little tasks, I get my own *office?*

Wow! My first day at college, and already things are clicking. Instantly, I have been separated from the hoi polloi. Now I won't have to be among the huddled masses of freshmen all studying together in the reference room. No. Now I get my own *office,* in which I can truly focus on . . . *differentiation.*

"It's gratifying to see how much you've thinned out in these few weeks," the T.A. began. "Some more thinning out to be done, I'd warrant. . . .

"Differentiation! Take a function; graph it. Slope! Slope of straight line equals 'rise over run.' Remember? Good. Slope of *curve* equals slope of line tangent to point on curve. *Tangent line* is line touching curve at one point. *Secant line* is line touching curve at *two* points.

"As second point of secant line approaches approaches approaches first point of tangent line, secant line approaches

$$f(x) = x^2$$
$$f'(x) = 2x$$

approaches approaches tangent line. Thus *slope* of secant approaches approaches approaches *limit* of slope of tangent—approaches *limit* of slope of tangent.

"Thus, if we take the function, say, *f(x)* equals *x²*, we arrive at the *derivative* of that function, equal to *2x*. . . . Function: *x²*. *Derivative* of function: *2x*. Because *second* point point point approaches *first* point, and secant line approaches approaches tangent line, and slope of secant approaches approaches approaches *limit* of slope of tangent—approaches *limit* of slope of tangent. . . .

"It's that simple."

At the end of class, everyone again went streaming out of the lecture hall looking as if they knew exactly what the grad-student T.A. had been talking about. I, however, had my questions. I mean, I *kind* of got what he was talking about. I knew what a tangent line was: it's a line that grazes me at one point. And I knew what a secant line was: it's a line that goes through me at *two* points. I just didn't know what *either* had to do with *2x*. I saw no connection between them!

Fortunately, the T.A. was still there at his lectern, gathering his papers together.

I said, "Excuse me, sir, but I was just wondering if I could ask you a little q—"

He said, "What? You wanted to ask me a . . . *question?*"

I said, "Oh no, I'd never ask you a *question.* No, sir. I'd never ask you a *question.* No. Rather, I was hoping to, uh, *posit* to you (if you will) kind of a— a— a tiny little, uh . . . *query.* . . . Oh, never mind."

As I slipped out of Fine Hall, I could see the huge line of all the other freshmen who, like me, had put off taking the swimming test until this very last possible day. As my line snaked towards the swimming pool building, I was thinking, Why do *I* have to do this? What could this possibly have to do with me becoming a brilliant mathematician? Did *Einstein* have to take a swimming test? . . . Well, he probably did, actually—he went to Princeton. Perhaps Einstein had some older brother far more brilliant than he—say, Ludwig. But Ludwig could only swim *half* a lap . . . so we never heard of him.

The swimming pool building had been built with funds donated not by a wealthy alumnus, but by the *mom* of a wealthy alumnus. The alumnus himself had drowned. His mother had then donated this money to Princeton so that thenceforth, anyone who drowned would do so in an enclosed area.

As I got closer and closer to the pool, I started flashing back to all my childhood traumas relating to swimming pools. Especially at summer camp. Even at math camp. Math camp! You'd think at math camp you'd be safe to do your little, nerdy equations. But no—even at math camp there were these sadistic, blond, musclebound counselors going, "C'mon, Joshy, jump in the water."

"No. I'm never, ever going in the water. I guess if you want me to go in the water, you'll have to *throw* me in."

"Well, okay . . ." SPLASH!

"Waah! Waah! But I can't swim! *I can't swim!*"

And they fished me out, and I'm flopping along the side of the pool. "Waah! Waah!" And the counselor's going, "See, bet you're not frightened anymore!"

Grrr. . . .

So I'm standing at the edge of the Princeton pool, just trying to find the motivation within myself for getting into the water, making it to the other end and back, so that I may continue with my undergraduate career. Just trying to find that motivation within myself, when I hear from behind me this heavily accented voice: "You have a choice, you know. You don't have to swim. You can always . . . *sink.*"

And I saw this elderly woman coming towards me. In her mid-seventies, I'd say, but still very vigorous looking. She had a circa-1920s swimsuit on, and a swimming cap pulled down tight, and these bushy white eyebrows. Very fierce. She walked up to me.

"Hello, young man. I am Gospozha Dolenko. I am your swimming instructor. Yes, I have tenure—yes! Young man, I see you are nervous. Don't worry. If something happens to you in the water, Gospozha Dolenko will come save you. How about that?"

And she started to walk away. I said, "Well, thanks—I mean, *spaciba.*"

She said "*Pazholusta*— WAIT! What did you just say?!"

"I said, '*Spaciba.*'"

"Where did you *learn* that?"

"Well, I took Russian in high school."

"They don't teach Russian in *high school!*"

"Well, uh, then I did go to Russia and I spoke Russian with Russians."

"They don't speak Russian in *Russia!*"

"Well, uh, then where *do* they speak Russian?"

"Only in this swimming pool building. And one or two towns in France. And that's it! . . . Young man, come with me."

And she pulled me to a corner of the room—where, next to a big lifeguard chair, there was a table dominated by this huge samovar, from which she proceeded to pour us both glasses of steaming hot Russian tea!

"Young man, have you by chance read the great Russian literature?"

"Well, in high school we read some Tolstoy . . ."

"Tolstoy is not *Russian!*"

"Hmm. Well, I, uh, was *about* to say we also read some Dostoevsky."

"*HE'S* NOT—"

"No, I didn't think he'd be Russian, either. . . . Um, who *is* Russian?"

"Only *Pushkin,* the great Russian poet, young man."

And she lifted up from the table this slender little volume that was wrapped in plastic, I guess to protect it from the elements—

water, chlorine . . . And she opened it up to a particular page and handed it to me.

"Young man, *please*, read to me aloud this Pushkin poem."

"Uh . . . okay. . . . Well, the title of the poem is 'K——,' meaning, 'To' someone; it doesn't say to whom. Okay. Here's the first line: '*Ya pomnyu choodnuye mgnovyenye.*'"

"No no no no no. YA POMNYU CHOODNUYE MG-NOVYENYE."

"Okay, uh . . . '*Ya POMnyu*—'"

"No no no no no. YA POMNYU CHOODNUYE MGNOV-YENYE. *Say* it!"

"You know, there's still people *swimming* here. . . . Um, Gospozha Dolenko, perhaps if I could just *borrow* this book for a couple of days, so I could translate this poem for myself. Because I think maybe the problem is, this is in kind of—if you'll forgive me—kind of an *archaic* form of Russian that I'm not so familiar with. So perhaps when I *understand* it, I'll be able to come back and properly say it to you. . . ."

"No no no no no. You don't have to UNDERSTAND it! Just MEMORIZE, and SPIT IT BACK OUT."

"Wait. You're saying I don't really need to *understand*—"

"Just MEMORIZE, and SPIT IT BACK OUT. . . . Young man, think of the great Russian poets of old, declaiming from the center of a soccer stadium filled to the brim with poetry lovers. No amplification. Just say it—SAY it!"

"Hold on. You're saying, Don't need to understand. Can just memorize, and spit it back— Hmm. Excuse me."

Back in my office, I started working on this huge brainstorm. What if I could transfer what I had just learned from Gospozha Dolenko about Russian—what if I could transfer that to my problems with . . . calculus!

Yes! Because so far, in my calculus class, I haven't been *following* it—and I think I've let that hold me back. Maybe I've just been too hung up on *understanding* the math I've taken. I mean, I really felt I understood the math I took in grade school, in middle school and high school. But perhaps at this level, I don't *need* to understand it. Maybe *that's* why calculus is "the mathematics of change." What has changed is that from now on, I won't *understand* it!

I took my Thomas textbook, Volume 9,012, and I just memorized all the equations. I didn't know what any of the equations meant; I didn't know what any of the equations had to do with any of the *other* equations. I just memorized all the equations. Just stuffed and stuffed my head with equations. Just filled my head with equations. Just stuffed and filled and packed my head with equations. Filled and packed and stuffed my head with equations. Packed and packed and sqeezed my head with equations. Till finally it came time for the calculus midterm, and I— BRAAAAAAAGH!—spit it all back out! And I *aced* it!!!

And all during the next calculus lecture, I could not focus on what the grad-student T.A. was saying—I was so obsessed with what would happen at the *end* of class, when we all got to pick up our graded exams. You see, that had been one of my very few joys back in high school. I'd had so few dates, really. One of my

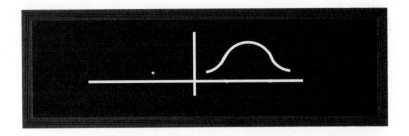

very few pleasures was to gaze and gaze upon my graded exams, with their bright red ink "100s." "Excellent work, Josh." "Check, check, check, check, check, check . . ." I was so obsessed with what would happen at the *end* of class that I didn't really see fit to focus on what the T.A. was going on about, in . . . *integration.*

"So—The Few, The Proud. . . .

"*Integration.* Many uses for integration. One use: calculating the area under a curve. Could be any curve. Could be *any* curve. I happen to have chosen the curve that represents . . . the grade distribution of your midterms.

"As you can see, a few of you are up here at the top. Most of you, in the middle. Some of you, at the bottom.

"Actually, *one* of you . . . all the way down . . . *there.* . . ."

And at that moment, something happened. At that moment I realized that even when I did try to focus on what the T.A. was saying, *I still could not understand him.* It was as if he had suddenly become one of the teachers in those Charlie Brown TV specials. You know, "Waaa waaa waaa waa waa waa wa. Wa wa wa.

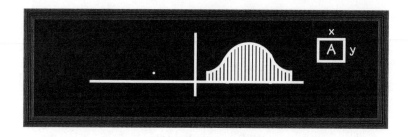

"*Wawagration.* Area. . . . Area within *rectangle:* x times y. Wa wa wa.

"Got it? Wa.

"Area under *curve:* inscribe rectangles under curve—

"Yes, Ms. Picouly, they *could* be circumscribed instead of inscribed—it would approach the same thing. They won't all understand it, though. But very good. Wa wa wa.

"Number of rectangles: *n.* Base of each rectangle: *1 over n.* As *n* approaches infinity, *1 over n* approaches *1 over infinity.*

"Wa wa wa.

"Thinner and thinner rectangles, more and more rectangles.

"Wa wa wa waaa.

"An infinite number of infinitely thin rectangles.

"Waa wa waa wa.

"Fill in the curve! Fill in the curve!

"Wa wa wa wa wa!

"Area within rectangle! Area under curve!

"Waaa waaa waaa waa waa waa wa. Wa wa wa wa *waa* wa wa.

"It's that simple."

At the end of class I was at the end of the, by now, thankfully very short line to pick up our graded midterms. I was the last in line, so I picked up the very last midterm—my own. . . .

58?!! I thought I *aced* this!

5-8. I *know* those numerals. But never before have they been presented to me *in this order.* . . . *58*—on my calculus *midterm?!*

"Um, excuse me, sir! I just wanted to—"

"WHAT? You think I've made an *error?* It that it? You think I have erred in grading your . . . midterm?"

"Oh no, sir—no! I think *I* have erred. I have obviously erred *multiply:* I got a *58!* No, sir. The thing is, I *studied,* sir. I memorized all the equations in the textbook. Now, I *did* notice, while I was taking the exam, that all the problems in the exam were just *slightly* different from the examples in the textbook. But I was sure that if I just applied the same, uh, *stuff,* it would work out pretty much the same way. . . . But it *didn't* work out. No, sir. It worked out wrong. It worked out *multiply* wrong! . . . And I guess what I'm saying is—you're the only instructor I know of on the whole campus who does not have office hours. And I was wondering if you could take, like, some extra time to give me some special . . . *help.*"

"HELP? You want me to . . . *help* you? And what is it that you think I am trying to do now, if not *help* you. I am trying to *help* you make what, to me, would seem a very simple decision. Mr. Kornbluth, you saw the grades on the midterm. You're all the way down there. You're . . . that . . . *point!* . . . The choice should seem obvious. You should give up my calculus class. In fact, give up mathematics. Forever. Mr. Kornbluth, *you have hit . . . the wall.*"

"*Huh?* J-just because I got a lousy grade on my midterm? . . . You know, at this moment, sir, I am not able to articulate to you exactly why what you just said to me is totally ridiculous. But I'm gonna go away and get it together and then—believe me, sir— I'm gonna come back and explain it to you!"

I staggered out across campus. Everyone I encountered was in a state of mild post-midterm euphoria. There they stood, in little clumps and clusters in doorways. Having conversations. Having— I could tell—very *intelligent* conversations. Because these were ob- viously very smart people. They were true scholars; they belonged here. You could touch them; they were palpable; they were *there.*

I, however—felt myself to be . . . *flickering.*

What am I going to do? . . . I know! I'll go see my one kind- of friend on campus: Dean Pablo Lucci.

But when I got to Nassau Hall, the entranceway was blocked by a picket line organized by the People's Front for the Liberation of Southern Africa. They were going round and round on this picket line, chanting this same chant over and over:

Princeton divest! (Uh-huh!)
Just like the rest! (Uh-huh!)
And if you don't (And if you don't)
We will not rest! (We will not rest!)

And I totally agreed with them, of course: I believed in divest- ing stocks in corporations that did business in apartheid South Africa. The problem I had was with their *name*—the People's

Front for the Liberation of Southern Africa—which I felt to be a tad, mmmm, *pretentious*. "People's Front": I mean, at Princeton, we couldn't really say we were *the people*. Nor could we truthfully assert that we were *at the front*. True, we had an excellent crew team—and eventually they could get there. But really, not the people and not the front.

Still, I'd been trained since birth never to cross a picket line. So for a while I joined with them, chanting right along.

Princeton divest! (Uh-huh!)
Just like the rest! (Uh-huh!)
And if you don't (And if you don't)
We will not rest! (We will not rest!)

And then, after a few times around, I went off very discreetly on a tangent into the building.

"Uh, excuse me, Dean Lucci?"

"Oh hi, Josh, come in, sit down. I'll be right with you. I'm just a bit preoccupied, at this moment, with those chanting students down there. Have you heard them? . . . Oh no, Josh, I'm totally in sync with them *politically*—really, I am. It's just . . . that chant itself.

"Josh, if you, like me, have any sense of poetry, don't you think it would get to you? I mean, hearing the same chant, over and over, under my window. Minute after minute . . . hour after hour . . . day after day. Their parents spending hundreds of thousands of dollars for them to attend this august institution. And the

only chant they can come up with is one that rhymes 'rest' with
. . . 'rest'? . . . Listen, Josh, listen!"

Princeton divest! (Uh-huh!)
Just like the rest! (Uh-huh!)
And if you don't (And if you don't)

Dean Lucci couldn't help himself. He pulled open the window and
yelled down: "WE'LL BUILD A NEST!!!"

Sighing, he shut the window. "Thanks, Josh. Thanks for in-
dulging me. . . . And now, how can I help *you*? (Hey, have you
been working out with that arm? I notice it's quite bigger than the
other one. . . .) Oh, wait, Josh—don't tell me. You don't have to
say a word. I know why you're here. You WANT TO DO MATH.
You want me to let you drop all your non-math courses. (No,
Josh, don't even say a word.) And you know something, Josh, I
really shouldn't let you do this—but I know how much you love
your math, so I'm gonna let you do it. Just take this drop form,
have all your non-math instructors sign it, bring it back to me,
and I'll let you drop all your non-math classes. How about that?"

I took the drop form.

"Uh . . . thanks, Dean Lucci. Actually, though, I just came here
to kind of . . . talk. . . . Oh, never mind."

As I drifted through campus with my drop form, I was thinking: "I can't drop calculus! I mean, if I drop calculus, it'll be a
rocky road to mathematical greatness. . . . No. I think I have now
reached the point where I must avail myself of one of those

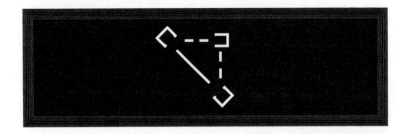

resources they have for extremely troubled students like me. I must take myself to the . . . Counseling Center."

And that's what I did. I went to the Counseling Center. I was assigned a counselor, and I'm sure he was very nice, very therapeutic. (I mean, he had a nice beard, so he must have been very therapeutic.) But it was no use, because by this point I just had math math math on the brain. So the whole time he was talking, all I could think about—all I was obsessed with—was the geometric arrangement of chairs in his office.

Because I'm sitting in *this* corner, right? And he's sitting in the opposite corner. Then there's this unoccupied chair in the *other* corner. And all I can think about as he's talking to me is, "He sat me along the hypotenuse! We are as far away from each other as two people could possibly be. Why didn't he sit me along the *base* of the triangle? Wouldn't that be a lot more intimate, a lot more therapeutic?"

So as he kept talking, I kept eyeing the unoccupied chair along the base of the triangle. And then he noticed that I kept eyeing the unoccupied chair—so even though he kept talking, *he* started eyeing the unoccupied chair. So our eyelines were both, you know, approaching the limit of the unoccupied chair from both directions—approaching, but never quite *reaching* it. . . .

Finally I stood up and said, "Look, sir, I'm sure what you're saying to me is very therapeutic, but I really gotta—uh . . . I gotta hit the pool."

Which of course was the last thing I *really* wanted to do. But it was, in fact, true: I had my weekly, mandatory swimming lesson. (The fact that I had not yet been *in* the pool shouldn't really mean anything at this point. . . .)

When I got to the pool, it was totally unoccupied except for Gospozha Dolenko herself. She was merrily swimming on her back, occasionally spitting out water like a happy porpoise.

"Oh, hello, Yasha! So you finally show up. . . . What am I doing in the pool? Well, I figure that since these are nominally *swimming* lessons, at least one of us should be in the *water*—no? So come on, Yasha, why don't you make yourself useful? Why don't you recite to me the last stanza of that Pushkin poem. *Y sertzye byotsa ve upayenye*—"

"No, Gospozha Dolenko, I can't do it."

"Oh, come on, Yasha—just *say* it: *Y sertzye byotsa*—"

"No, you see, that's just the problem, Gospozha Dolenko. What you told me *doesn't work*. It doesn't work for learning Russian. And it *certainly* doesn't work for learning math. Because—you know something? Thanks to what you told me, I have just now for the first time actually *flunked a math exam!* So it doesn't work for Russian; it doesn't work for math. And if you

$$10x = 9.\cancel{999}\ldots = 0$$
$$-\ \underline{x = 0.\cancel{999}\ldots = 0}$$
$$9x = 9 \quad \xcancel{\ } = 0$$
$$x = 1$$

think it's gonna teach me how to *swim,* I think you're wrong. Because I just learned something in math class: I learned that I am a *point!* That's right—a *point,* Gospozha Dolenko. And a point has no mass and no volume, SO HOW COULD IT FLOAT? All a point has is an *address.* And *my* address is in the bottom sub-basement of the physics building, and that's where I'm gonna stay until I figure out this shit!!"

Back in my office. . . . Okay. Where did I go wrong? I went wrong from the moment when I did not understand . . . THIS: *0.999 . . .* equaling *1.* I did not understand that. And then, in my stupidity and ignorance, I thought: "Well, perhaps I need not *understand* it; perhaps I can just *memorize* everything and spit it back out." THIS WAS A HUGE MISTAKE! But it's a mistake that it's not too late to correct. For now I'm going to *prove* to myself why *0.999 . . .* equals *1.* And once I've proved that, I'm sure everything else will start to fall into place.

But how do I prove it?

Okay, let's get back to first principles. I used to be *good* at math, didn't I? Like back in high school, in algebra. . . . Okay, let's try it *algebraically.*

$$0.9999999999 \quad 9$$

9 = 0		
18 = 9	= 0	
27 = 9	= 0	
36 = 9	= 0	
99 = 18	= 0	

Let's say that *x* is equal to *0.999* . . . Now multiply the whole thing by, say, *10*. So we have *10x*. Now when you multiply *0.999* . . . by *10,* you just move the decimal point over—so *10x* would be equal to *9.999* . . . Now let's *subtract.* See? *10x* minus *x* is *9x*. And those nines cancel each other out.

So *9x* is equal to *9*. Now divide by *9,* and *x* equals . . . *1*??

Did I just *solve* it? Did I just Solve The Problem? . . . And if I *have* Solved The Problem, why do I still feel so . . . queasy?

I bet there's something really simple and obvious that I overlooked. I'd better check my calculations by Casting Out Nines.

Okay. So all these nines on the first and second lines cast out to . . . *0*. And *0* minus *0* equals *0*—which should be equal to . . . *1*?? No—SHIT!!

Okay, okay, let's go back to *really* first principles: *counting.* What was, say, *9* to me when I was a little boy? *9* was nine of my "counting blocks." I'd push them together. Push! *Push!* . . .

So this is what I'm gonna do: I'm gonna take *0.999* . . .—but instead of doing that "three dot" shortcut thing, I'll just keep going—*0.999999*—I mean, I have all day; I have all the time in the world, really—*0.999999999*.

Okay, now I'm going to focus on the first *9*, right after the decimal point. I'm going to empathize with that *9*, at the very front of the line. All the other nines *pushing* on it, *pushing*—the line of nines getting longer and longer, stretching out into infinity: an infinitely long line of nines. Now, *our 9*—all it has holding it back from jumping into the "units" place is this little, tiny decimal point here. But *meanwhile,* it has all these other nines behind it— pushing, shoving, jostling—an unruly, infinitely long line of nines—pushing, pushing, *pushing* . . . Our nine is holding back all those other nines—it's trying to hold them back—till finally it *can't* hold them back any longer—so it leaps over and becomes . . . *1??* No, *9.* It's still a *9!* FUCK!!

Okay, wait. Maybe my problem here is simply one of *orientation.* Sure! Maybe I've just been orienting myself improperly.

Right. So now, let's start with *9* again—but this time, instead of going out horizontally, we'll just make our nine a little *taller.* A little thinner, a little taller. Taller and thinner. Taller and thinner. Taller, taller, taller—till IT'S KIND OF LIKE A *1!*

Oh, that's stupid! STUPID!

Hmmm . . .

You know what my problem is? I think it's that I've always grossly overestimated my self-worth. Sure! Because look: back when I was a little boy, my dad told me I was going to be the most brilliant mathematician who ever lived. At the time, I was nine years old. . . . If I had just bothered to cast myself out, I would have seen I was just . . . *0.*

Now, in a few weeks, I'm going to turn *18*—which will add

up to 9, which will cast out to 0. Then I'll be 27: I'll still be working on my thesis—it won't be going well—it'll add up to 9, which will cast out to 0. Thirty-six—I'll be on my second marriage, which will be *failing*: cast out to 0. On and on until I'm totally decrepit: 99, which will add up to 18, which will add up to 9, which will cast out to 0. I will *always* be 0. I'll *always always always*—

Oh, wait.

Maybe my problem is that I've been multiplying 9 by numbers that are *too small*. Yeah! Maybe, instead, I should multiply 9 by some . . . BIG FUCKING NUMBER.

That's it. I'll take 9 and I'll multiply it by, like, *everything!* 1, 2, 3, 4, 5, 6, 7 (in deference to Crowder, I'll leave out 8), 9.

Okay, now multiply. 9 times 9 is 81, carry the 8. 9 times 7 is 63, plus 8 is 71, carry the 7. 9 times 6 is 54, plus 7 is 61, carry the 6. 9 times 5 is 45, plus 6 is 51, carry the 5. 9 times 4 is 36, plus 5 is 41, carry the 4. 9 times 3 is 27, plus 4 is 31, carry the 3. 9 times 2 is 18, plus 3 is 21, carry the 2. 9 times 1 is 9, plus 2 is 11. 111111111. We've got a lot of ones here—maybe we're closing in on something! . . .

But wait. WAIT! Look what I've done! For the first time in

years, I have actually *written down the numbers that I've carried.* I'm weak! WEAK! WEAK! WEAK! WEAK! WEAK!

I can't do it. *I have hit the wall.* . . . . What do you think of that, Enrico?

Enrico?

His tank light had burned out. When did *that* happen? Sometime in the last few weeks, maybe? I scanned the murky depths of the tank, where Enrico usually liked to hang out. No sign of him!

Enrico? *Enrico?*

What are you doing *all the way up there?* And why have your little red eyes turned . . . black?

I fished him out. You know, fella, the one mistake you made was letting me be the guy who watched over you.

The cyclotron room was empty. I briefly thought of putting him inside the cyclotron, but I didn't really see what that would achieve. . . .

The cooling tank! Yes. Lots of crisp, clear water.

I put Enrico in the cooling tank, watched him float up to the surface. Well, guy, I'm afraid that's the best I can offer in terms of a decent burial . . .

I stink.

I gotta get . . . clean.

It was easy for me to slip into the swimming pool building. (*Ewwww,* chlorine!) The surface of the pool was totally still; I could see it illuminated by the moonlight diffracted in through the window grates. The surface of the water, totally still—it looked like a wall of . . . sheet metal. I went over to the aluminum ladder, began climbing it.

I got to the level of the diving board but then, on an impulse, I kept going—*up*. Higher and higher . . . Oh, and I hate heights —and I hate the water. Higher and higher . . . I must be getting close to the ceiling by now! Higher and higher—till finally I reached the level of the high diving platform.

I walked out onto the platform, stepped all the way over the edge. . . . So high up! You can hardly smell the chlorine from here. . . .

I'm sorry. . . .

I leaned out into the void, and I began to . . . PLUNGE!

And as I plunged, my head, being the largest and heaviest part of my anatomy, quickly took the lead. Plunging towards the surface of the pool. . . .

Suddenly this image formed in my head! This image of the distance between myself and the water being constantly bi-sected—being constantly, constantly bisected. Of my getting closer and closer to, but never actually quite *reaching* that limit of the wall of water!

I thought, "That's *it!!* I'LL NEVER HIT THE WATER! I'LL NEVER HIT THE WATER! I'LL NEVER HIT THE—"

WHOOOOOSH!!! . . .

Where am I? . . . Cool tiles? . . . I'm at the bottom of the pool!

Oh, it's nice here. I think I like it here. I must be a . . . bottom feeder. I'm going to stay here forever. Yeah! I'm going to stay down here forever, and ever, and—

Wait! Something's happening! Where's the floor going? I'M RISING!

But wait! I don't want to rise! I want to stay at the bottom of the pool forever and ever! I don't want to rise! But I'm rising—higher and higher . . . higher and higher . . . until I *burst* through the surface of the water!

BUT I CAN'T SWIM!! I CAN'T SWIM!! *I CAN'T SWIM!!*

And yet, I'm staying up!

I'm floating! . . . I'm floating? . . . I'm floating. . . .

You know, there's a function in math. A function that even those of us who long ago hit the wall can still understand. It's called the *identity function.* In the identity function, x, the variable, goes into the function machine. But instead of getting transformed into y, instead, miraculously, it reemerges as x itself. Sounds weird, I know. Doesn't even sound like a function. But it is. You can graph it. On the graph, the identity function first appears as a line—a line rising slowly, perhaps even reluctantly, from out of the murky depths. But then, at the very moment it crosses the x-axis—at that precise instant—it becomes . . . a point. A single point. Floating in a sea of possibilities. A point.

I stared at the waves reflected on the ceiling. I had no idea how I was going to get back to the side of the pool.

But for now, I was content to let the water carry me.

haiku tunnel

We've tried to screen this audience very carefully.

But just in case any lawyers somehow made it through, I just want to say that this story I'm about to tell you—which deals, in large part, with attorneys—is totally fictional. Is that clear?

I *made it up*—okay?

Like, in this story there's going to be this big corporate attorney named "Bob Shelby." I invented him. He's not based on anyone. In fact, after I invented Bob Shelby, I then changed his name from something *completely different* to . . . "Bob Shelby." So you see how far from reality this all is?

Now in this story, Bob Shelby is going to have a secretary: "Josh." And again, because this "Josh" has my name—and looks like me and sounds like me—you may be tempted to think that he *is* me. But nothing could be further from the truth.

For example, perhaps in the course of this story "Bob" will give his secretary—"me"—some eighty-five or so very important letters to mail out. And perhaps in the course of this story those letters won't get out, like, totally immediately. So again, I just want to stress— In fact, I don't even care so much about lawyers, but if there's anyone here from Personnel . . .

I, the *real* me, am an excellent secretary.

But in the *story*, "Bob" gave "me" about eighty-five very important letters to mail out. And I didn't.

And I think Bob had every reason to think that I *would* mail them out. Because I had just gone perm for Bob—I had just gone *perm*. . . . The previous week I'd been a *temp* for Bob. And in *that* week, everything Bob gave me to do I did *right away*—because that week I was a *temp*. And when I'm a temp, I'm great!

I mean, I show up for work on time. I never use the phone for personal calls. (Granted, it often takes me a few days to figure out *how* to use the phone for personal calls—but what I'm telling you is, even if I knew, I wouldn't . . . when I'm a temp.)

When I'm a temp, I take no more than an hour for lunch each day. And when my boss is in a crisis, I make sure to arrange my features to reflect the gravity of the situation.

And when my boss is in a *good* mood, I chuckle apprecia-tively at his jokes. When I'm a temp.

And I came from a great temp agency, too: UNIFORCE.

"Hello! I'm from UNIFORCE. Take my cape. Show me to my computer. There's your document. Next! . . . I'm from UNI-FORCE!"

I was so proud to be a temp from UNIFORCE. Just the name alone filled me with pride. I was sure all the *other* temps from UNIFORCE felt that same pride. . . . But in all the millions of law firms I worked at downtown in San Francisco, I never met one other temp from UNIFORCE. I started to think: maybe *I'm* the "UNI"?

I'd ask other temps, "Where are *you* from?"

"I'm from the Phil Agency."

"I'm from the Sue Agency."

"I'm from the Frank—"

Did you know there's a one-to-one ratio of temp agencies to humans? Were you aware of this?

"I'm from the Lucrezia Agency."

"I'm from the Borgia—"

"I'm from UNIFORCE!"

"Then you must be Josh," said Marlina D'Amore.

Marlina was the head secretary of the Tax Group at Schuyler & Mitchell, an enormous downtown law firm with an unfortunate acronym that I'd been assigned to. Marlina was a small, intense woman of Slavic descent with raven black hair and piercing dark eyes, and she wore on her bicep this kind of snake-bracelet that sort of made her look like a warrior.

She said, "Welcome, Josh. Welcome to S&M. Allow me to show you to your room."

I thought: "Oooohhh." Because you don't usually get a room when you're a temp, you know. A lot of times it's: "We'll turn this bucket upside down, you sit on that."

As she escorted me down the hallway to my room, we passed all these secretaries who'd obviously been there forever, but for some reason they didn't get rooms; they just had desks in the hallway. And as we passed each secretary in turn, Marlina introduced me to them. I remember the first one, Mindy, was working way too busily to look up when we were introduced. The second one, Darlene, was cursing at a laser printer—which was making kerchunking sounds back at her. (After we passed her desk, Marlina explained to me, "Darlene's from New York." Oh.) DaVonne, with her nice bangs—she looked up, smiled sweetly at me, and went right back to work.

DaVonne, Darlene . . . One of my great joys in working downtown is secretarial names. They're so beautiful. I count my own: Jah-shuuuu-aaah. In the years I've worked down there, these are some of my favorite secretaries I worked with: Aline, Eileen, Darlene, Charlene, Carlina, Marlina, Yvonne, Yvonette, Yvonetta, Clifford, . . . Aurora. Aur-or-ra!

Compare those to *lawyer* names—a totally different beast. In the same period of time, these are the attorneys I've worked for: Bob. Bob. Bob. Bob, Bob, Bob, Bob. Jim, Jim, Jim, James, Jim. Nate the Third. Dave, Dave, Dave, Dave, Dave, Dave. Bob.

As she took me down the hallway to my room, Marlina explained to me, "You know, Josh, you're not going to be working for just *any* attorney—you're going to be working for the top guy here in the Tax Group!"

I gasped! Because, you see, I hadn't done my taxes for seven years. So it was kind of a sore spot with me.

She said, "There's your room, Josh. Work hard. Enjoy." And she walked away.

Now, what she'd pointed at *looked* like a *desk*. It looked like *a desk in the hallway*. But she had called it my "room"—so it must be a room.

I looked at the side of the desk. It had a little plaque: "ROOM 1525A." So it's *definitely* a room. . . . Kind of an Orwellian usage of the language. (I say that mostly because I've never read Orwell, so I kind of get a kick out of saying it.)

I walked into my "room," making sure not to bump into any "walls." I sat down at my desk and I took stock. Right away I like to take stock. You want to see what supplies might be . . . useful— what supplies might be, uh, *stealable,* in any way. (Uniball Micro pens—my own personal weakness. I could go on and on about my love for Uniball Micros. Let me just say this much: they never explode in your pocket like Bic pens. They don't. They just *expire* one day—and so gracefully! They're like the Camille of pens.)

I took stock of my desk. There was no stock to take! Someone had practiced a scorched-desk policy on my desk! All I could find rattling around in one of the empty drawers—I found this lonely, forlorn little envelope moistener. You know, with a squeeze tube and a sponge tip? It looked kind of frightened to be out of its drawer, so I put it back in.

Up on the bulletin board there was just one thing: an internal Schuyler & Mitchell memo—with, you know, "S & M" emblazoned at the top. The memo was dated December 31, 11 p.m. A memo dated 11 p.m. on New Year's Eve!

The memo began, "Dear Helen, . . ."

I gasped!

You see, I'd been *living* with a Helen. I had just *split up* with a Helen. And it was amazing that we'd lasted the year that we lasted, because we were so different. Helen grew up in the town of Larkspur, in Marin County, and she's kind of a mountain-bicycler. *I* grew up in New York, and I'm more of a—a *worrier*, I guess. . . . So we each brought our strengths into the relationship.

Helen would come back after riding three billion miles on her mountain bike. She'd walk in and say, "I'm getting more and more buff!" And I'd say, "I'm getting more and more . . . nervous."

And yet, as the months went by—I can't account for it—

but, despite our differences, we started to get . . . close. You know, intimate. It got to the point that there was no telling how intimate we could get—so I moved out. And I told her under no circumstances to call me, and she hadn't called me, and I was waiting.

"Dear Helen," the memo began. "As the new year rapidly approaches, I thought I would outline for you your duties as my new secretary. . . ."

This was followed by eleven and a half *single-spaced* pages of instructions! One glance at those and I decided right away: *I need to find the coffee room.* Because, you know, coffee's a friend. It's been documented. It picks you up, it lets you down. It's a pal.

And as I made my way back up the hallway in search of the coffee room, I passed all these secretaries I had just been introduced to. Now *none* of them looked up or even acknowledged me in any way—which a couple of years earlier, when I was just starting out, would have hurt my feelings. But by this point I had learned that—especially at these huge firms downtown—they get so many of us temps going in and out of their hallways, many of us lasting only *seconds*. It's like, we all must have billions of helpful bacteria in our intestines, but if you took the time to meet and greet each one of them, that's your whole life right there. I understand that.

In fact, I was even *glad* that no one was talking to me, because at this particular stage of my post-Helen melancholia, I was transferring most of my affections to . . . my bed—my little single bed in my new studio apartment. I would *lust* for my bed during the day. I'd think, "Ooh, I'm going to get home and rip off my clothes and leap under the covers—it'll be *just us.*" And I would just as soon that people not interrupt my reveries about my bed by talking to me. That's fine.

I got my cup of coffee and brought it back to my desk. A few minutes later, Bob Shelby emerged from his office.

Bob Shelby—middle-aged, successful attorney. Have I painted the picture for you? Is it vivid? Good.

"You must be Josh!"

"You must be Bob!"

"Come into my office, Josh!"

"Okay, Bob!"

So we seemed to have a rapport.

As I followed him into his office, he started rattling off these very efficient-sounding phrases, I guess telling me what my duties were going to be. I didn't *listen* to him, of course. No insult to Bob. I had just learned, through countless first days of temp assignments, that I cannot absorb all that information at once. I can't. So I just nod and smile.

I don't know if you saw, about eleven years ago, there was this *Nova* episode on PBS where they filmed moms with their newborn infants, talking to their infants? And then, when they slowed the film way down, you could actually see the infants nodding and smiling—in all the right places! So it's innate with us. And I trust it.

So as Shelby chattered on about . . . *whatever,* I nodded and smiled—burping occasionally—and looked around his spacious office.

Right away, of course, I saw the obligatory family photo. This tells you right away: Shelby has sex with women, and he raises children. Which of course are the two prerequisites for doing tax law—I think we all understand that.

He had a "stand-up desk"—a desk he would stand up at! This is so in case an urgent tax matter came up, he could go, "I'll be right there!" VROOM—and he's out the door! Doesn't have to push himself back from a *conventional* desk, get up, go running around the desk—waste perhaps several unbillable seconds that way. No—just . . . *right out!*

By the way, I don't mean to imply that Shelby would actually pick up the phone. The Shelbys of the world do not pick up the phone. A big, important attorney . . . if he picked up the phone, his lips would be . . . right by the mouthpiece. Halfway across the world, the guy he's talking to—say, Bill—picks up *his* phone. His lips—*also* right by the mouthpiece. . . . They could be construed as kissing. And these big-time, successful attorneys do not kiss publicly. I've never even seen them *hug*—which is weird, since they're "partners." But they don't. No—what they have are . . . speakerphones:

"Hello, Bill! Yes, it's me. No, I'm not touching anything. I *swear* I'm not touching anything. . . . Uh, are *you* touching anything? . . . Good. Okay, let's get down to work, then. Five hundred million! . . . Seventy-nine billion! . . . Four hundred seventy-nine point six billion trillion quadrillion! . . ."

I took my first pile of work from Shelby and brought it out to my desk, where my phone was ringing—which was a little weird, since I didn't even know what my number was yet.

I picked up the phone. "Hello?"

"HELLO??? Is this JOSH???"

"Um, yeah."

"You're Bob Shelby's new secretary, right???"

"Well, I, uh, I'm *temping* for him."

"Josh, you don't know me. My name is—HELEN!!! I'm Bob Shelby's *previous* secretary—or, should I say, *victim??!*"

"Uh-huh . . ."

"Josh, have you seen that memo yet? When I got that memo, I walked right into his office. I said, 'Bob, you don't need a *secretary,* you need another *wife.*' . . . Josh, Shelby may *seem* like an okay guy. Does he?"

"Yeah, he does."

"Well, HE ISN'T! Mark my words well, my new friend. Beneath that calm, placid exterior, Bob Shelby is . . . EEEEEEEEVIL! EEEEEEEEVIL! BEWARE!!"

So this is what I decided: I decided that as long as I was going to be working for Bob Shelby, I'd work *really hard*—just on the off-chance that he *was* Satan. . . . You know, you'd want to make a good impression.

And the next day, after lunch, Marlina D'Amore cornered me in the coffee room. She said, "Jo-o-osh, Bob Shelby really likes you. Have you ever considered going . . . *perm?*"

I think I must have grabbed a countertop for support. It wasn't that I was thrown by the idea of going perm for the Prince of Darkness. No, it wasn't, because—believe me—I've worked for worse: Young Litigators on Crack, say: "Josh, come into my office, talk to me till dawn—I'll pay you double. . . ." I mean, at least Satan would be secure in his own power—and that's a plus.

No, what *terrified* me was the very vivid memory I had—that every time I had been persuaded to go perm, right after that, weird shit started happening. To me. Shit like the eighty-five letters that don't go out.

And Marlina was going, "Jo-o-osh, what about it? What about it?" You should have seen her eyes: they were desperate. It's like she was saying, "We must feed more meat to the dragon, or he will destroy the village!!"

I said, "I'm sorry, Marlina, I'm sorry. But I, uh, don't go perm on my first week."

And then, I don't know what it was. Maybe it's because we're both Slavic by descent. But it was like she could look right into my soul at that moment and she could see my weak spot, and she went right for it.

She said, "Now, Jo-o-osh . . . you go perm, and the firm will cover your . . . *psychotherapy.*"

And I can remember waking up on Monday morning and thinking, "Wow! My first conscious moment as a perm at S&M!" I paused a moment to consider the significance of this event—and when I woke up again, it was about 8:10. I had twenty minutes to get in to work. Luckily, I live right near BART, our subway system. So I got in to work on time. In fact, I was two minutes early: it was 8:28 when I arrived at the massive "Todd Building."

That's the name of the building I work in—the Todd Building. You *know* it's called the Todd Building because it says it on the ground right before you walk in: "Todd Building."

I was so nervous about going perm yet again, I decided I would try to humanize my office environment any way I could. So I decided I would try to think of the Todd Building not as being named after some wealthy Todd family, but rather, after a guy named Todd. A surfer, maybe.

"Hey there, Todd!"

"Yo, Josh!"

I mean, we didn't *say* that, but I *thought* it and it relaxed me, made me feel better.

And when I got up to my floor—the 15th floor—all the secretaries came up to me! "Welcome, Josh! Welcome to the S&M family! Understand you're perm now! Welcome! Welcome! Welcome!"

They're coming up and welcoming me; the whole previous week, when I'd been a temp, they had totally ignored me. I thought, "Why do I suddenly reflect light?" It was quasi-mystical. They even invited me to a birthday party one of them was having after work. Great!

And the first day you go perm at S&M, it's fun because you don't have to *work,* really. You just go to orientation meetings all day. They give you your benefits packets, and show you slide shows introducing you to various S&M practices and procedures you might want to follow at some point.

After work I went to this place I'd written down the address for, for this secretarial party. It was this place called Lascaux. Kind of an expensive, yuppie, postmodern restaurant-bar named after a famous French cave with paintings. (That do it for you?)

As I descended the stairs at Lascaux, I could see—beyond the sea of wandering, blank-eyed–looking young attorneys hoping to mate—all the secretaries from my group, the Tax Group. And as I approached the booth, I was sure that in the fifteen minutes be-tween when they were up at work and down here in this booth, some mad scientist must have injected each of them with . . . *life serum?*

Because up at work each of these secretaries, they're like au-tomatons: "Hello, yeah, yeah, uh-huh." But down here at the booth they're going, "HEY, MINDY, YOU OLD BAG, HOW OLD *ARE* YOU? HA HA HA HA HA."

"Well, I'm certainly glad I'm not still thirty-five, or I'd still be stuck with that fucking ex-husband of mine. How was *I* to know he was a mass-murderer? Well, at least *I* found Jesus. . . . BOTTOMS UP!"

DaVonne was passing this petition around the table. Turns out she's a rabid— I was about to say "rabid animal-rights activist" . . . but that's okay, actually; I like it.

Clifford was going on one of his Clifford things: "So I walked into Jack's office this morning. I said, 'Jack, I don't care if you're a partner—you owe me an apology. Because what you said to me on Friday, it ruined my weekend, Jack, and you owe me an apology.' I told him, 'Jack, I don't care if you're a partner. What you said to me on Friday, it ruined my weekend. It ruined my Saturday. It ruined my Sunday. That's my weekend, Jack, and you owe me an apology.' I went right up to him—I said, 'Jack, I don't *care* if you're a partner. You owe me an apology—'"

Then someone else at the table made the mistake of saying, "Well, he probably *did* owe you an apol—"

"Well, you're damn *right,* he did! And I told him, I said, 'I don't *care* if you're a *partner,* Jack—you owe me an apology. Because what you said to me on Friday, it ruined my weekend, Jack. I woke up Saturday morning, I was miserable. Nine to ten, miserable. Ten to eleven, worse. Eleven to twelve, even worse. Twelve to one, it was a little better—I was having lunch. One to two, worse. . . .'"

While this was going on, Denise, the receptionist—a very nice-looking woman in her sixties who's never spoken to me before—she leans over and goes, "Josh, you're new here. Be brutally frank with me. What do you think of the way I arrange the magazines?"

"Well, Denise, they look—they look very nicely arranged, up there in the lobby, very nice."

"Oh Josh, I thought you looked like a brighter boy than that. Haven't you noticed? I've been arranging them in a Jungian *mandala.*"

"Ah. Well. I . . . gotta go. . . ."

When I woke up the next morning, I felt—unaccountably—a little better than I had in a long time, a little less post-Helen depressed. So I needed to spend a few extra minutes in bed, just to savor that new feeling. That's just the way I operate. And as a result, I got in to work a little late. Maybe five minutes late. I don't think anyone noticed.

I went right into my "room" and started setting up my systems—because I'd inherited nothing. I put in some hanging folders—with some really, really pretty colored tabs. I got some loose timesheets that I found scattered around, and I put them together in a pile. And I three-hole-punched them. And I put them in a binder. And I put the binder up on a shelf. . . .

And then I thought, "Whew! I have been working very hard. I deserve some kind of reward about now." So I allowed myself the luxury of calling my best friend, Ed. I knew he wasn't going to be at home. I just wanted to leave on his answering machine my direct phone number at work.

And after I did that, I felt so good. I think it's because I knew that from that moment forward, at any time, someone out there, beyond my "room," beyond Todd, someone out in the world might think of me and actually be able to get through.

And that knowledge, I think, is what gave me the strength to go ahead and do . . . the computer shit that I had to do.

We have a VAX system at S&M, V-A-X—I don't know if it stands for anything—but what it seems to involve is that each of us has a terminal, but none of our terminals have any computer stuff *in* them. They're all connected via phone line to some central computer. No one knows where it is. We think maybe suburban Illinois, but no one knows why we think that.

And what this involves, you see, is: I have this really nice laser printer right next to my desk. But when I want to print something, I hit PRINT. And that instruction has to travel via phone line to, like, Joliet. And then a half-hour later, it comes stumbling back, crawls the last few agonizing inches into my printer, and commands it to eke out my one-paragraph memo.

That's how it works. It gets very complicated. Like, we all need passwords. Luckily we have this thing called "User Support"— which I know sounds like a jockstrap or drug rehab . . . but actually it's a computer help hotline. They're very polite to you, you know, because they're paid to be.

So I called them up, and they told me how to do my new, perm password: now that I wasn't a temp anymore, I couldn't use my old, temp password. They told me how to "initialize" my printer. Very important. First thing you do, after you turn on your terminal in the morning, is you initialize your printer. That involves telling that central computer in Joliet—you say, "When I say PRINT, I would like you to print . . . *here,* on the printer *right next to me.* The printer in *Baghdad,* say, would be . . . less convenient. So if it's all the same to you, *this* one would be nice. *This* one."

And while I had them on the line, I had this kind of hypothetical computer question that had been nagging at me, so I thought I'd ask them. I said, "Excuse me, but let's say, uh, *someone* wanted to input, into this computer, . . . a *novel.* And let's say he—or she!—didn't want anyone else to have access to this novel. Would this be possible?"

They said, "Oh yes, he or she could input his or her novel into his or her 'local directory.'"

Of course!! I'd forgotten: sometime in orientation, they'd told us that each of us has a local directory. Evidently, my local directory is "secure" to me—meaning no one else can get into it. I had not held that connection in my head—because as I said, I'm from New York, and in New York the words "local" and "secure" are not synonymous. If anything, in New York "local" connotes, "That which breaks down *every* stop." But "secure"? No.

So I tried it: I tried inputting my beloved would-be novel into my local directory. It seemed to go in fine. Great! Time for lunch.

My first few weeks working at a huge firm downtown, I need to go—it's not a *choice* thing—I need to go to McDonald's for lunch. Because I'm new in this huge place. I don't know who anyone is. I don't know where anything is. I need an hour, during each workday, when I know *exactly* what's going to happen to me. And McDonald's provides this.

As I was leaving McDonald's that day, I think what motivated me to return to work was the idea that when I got back up to my desk, perhaps the little red light on the side of my phone would be lit, indicating that someone had left me a message in my voice-mail box. But when I got back to my desk, the little red voice-mail light was out. So no one had called me. And I felt sad.

I set up some macros.

Macros are time-saving devices on the computer. I set up this macro that—when you hit the DO key, which activates the macro—what it does is, it generates the names of everyone I've ever met or heard of who by my age has not yet become wildly successful. Really cheers me up whenever I see that list—but you know, if every time I want to see it, I have to type it, that becomes very time consuming. That's why you have a macro! You hit the DO key, and the names come scrolling by. . . .

And when I woke up the next day, I felt even a little better—even a little less post-Helen depressed than I had the day before. So I needed to take a little *extra* time in bed, to savor that feeling. As a result I got in to work . . . maybe fifteen minutes late—which may not sound like a lot, but it is, if you're a legal secretary. Especially seeing as Marlina, being the head secretary, has her desk right at the beginning of the hallway. So you kind of have to run her gauntlet to get to *your* desk.

I tried whizzing past her desk at a supersonic-blur speed— vrrroooom!—so she wouldn't recognize me. As I whizzed past her desk, I couldn't tell if she recognized me or not, but out of the corner of my eye, I thought I saw her arm bracelet glow malevolently. So when I got to my desk, I instantly started typing really intensely, looking really intense. So if Marlina came by, she'd see I'm working way too intensely to be reprimanded at this time. . . . And then, after a few minutes went by, and Marlina didn't show up, I calmed down, turned on my computer, did some more systems work, and then Shelby brought me out his first dictation tape for me to do.

We used regular-sized cassettes for our dictation tapes at S&M, not those little wimpy mini-cassettes. And we had these transcribing machines that we operated with these cool pedals. You press the pedal and the tape goes forward. When you let go, the tape goes back so you can hear the last few words. It's really neat. I put in my first dictation tape from Shelby:

"Josh, take a memo. Mark it 'Personal and Confidential.' Dear Bill, uh, pursuant to Rev. Rule—"

I took my foot off the pedal. I was kind of phasing out. Let the tape go back to the beginning. I'll just start again.

"Josh, take a memo—"

Still kind of spacing out. I took my foot off the pedal, let it go back to the beginning.

Start again.

"Josh, take a—"

Again: "Josh, take a—" "Josh, take a—" "Josh, take a—"

Okay. "Josh, take a memo. Mark it 'Personal and Confidential.' Dear Bill, uh—" "Dear Bill, uh—" "Dear Bill, uh—" "Uhhh—" "Uhhh—" "Uhhh—" "Uhhh—" "Uhhh—" "Uhhh—" "Uhhh—" "Uhhh—"

My name is Josh!
I work at S&M!
If they don't do it to me,
I'm gonna do it to them!

"Uhhh—" "Uhhh—" "Uhhh—"

Whenever Shelby walked past my desk—particularly when I was fucking around—it sent these shivers through me. I never knew when his true Satanic colors were going to come out—his horns would pop out, and his tail. He'd go, "Jo-o-ossshhh . . ." Foom!!! Puff of smoke, and I'm a—a toadstool!

I'd better just type this memo. That's what I'm going to do—I'm just going to type this little memo. . . . But first, let's just see what happens when I pop in this Judas Priest cassette I brought in. Run it backwards, see if it really contains hidden Satanic messages: "Jo-o-ossshhh, stop fucking around and type the goddamn memo . . . Jo-o-ossshhh . . ."

AAAAAH!!!

And after lunch, Bob Shelby called me into his office. He said, "Josh, perhaps I'm missing something. But it seems to me that last week, when you were a temp, your productivity was very high. Whereas this week, as a perm, your productivity . . . low. Am I missing something? Is something . . . *wrong?*"

His politeness *terrified* me. I don't understand constant politeness—I don't. As I said, I'm from New York. In my tribe, people express what they think about you at every moment. Like, you go into the Famous Deli on Seventy-second Street. The waiter goes,

"You want a *blintz?* Am I *God?*" I understand that. The waiter hates me because . . . I *ordered.* That makes perfect sense within my culture. But the constant politeness of the Shelbys of the world, I don't know what's *underneath* that politeness—when whatever's underneath is gonna come up and *crush* me! . . .

I said, "I'm sorry, sir. I know my productivity's been down—but, you see, it's because I've been, um, um . . . Setting Up My Systems!"

And I could see his eyes instantly . . . relax. Accidentally, I had said The Right Thing. It's as if I'm wandering through the Everglades—all of a sudden I'm attacked by a giant crocodile. In my panic, I rub its tummy—and it goes to sleep.

"Systems, eh? I like that. But Josh, I hope you're done with those systems soon. Because I have this other project for you. It's another dictation tape. Has about eighty-five letters on it. Very important letters. Must go out right away. Okay?"

"Yes, sir! Yes, sir!"

I took the tape. I did not mess around. I put it in the transcriber. I typed up all eighty-five or so letters. I printed them out. He signed them. I Xeroxed them. I typed the envelopes. . . . But I did not . . . *mail* them.

And I think the reason *why* I did not mail them is because . . . mailing them would have been easy to do. And as a secretary, I need something easy to do—on standby, at all times. So that in case I should be given something *difficult* to do, something that might hurt my brain, I can at any time jump to the letters. And it's oh so soothing to mail letters—especially at S&M. You just seal the envelope and put it in the OUT box . . . seal the next envelope and put it in the OUT box . . . When you're done, eventually the mail clerk will come and take them all away and mail them.

I need something soothing like that, just waiting for me, in case I should lose my mind while doing *bills,* say.

Which is in fact what I did the rest of Wednesday afternoon: I did bills. And bills, of course, involve numbers and dollar signs. But for some reason, at S&M we have to put them in *column format.* I don't know if any of you have ever worked in column format—but you find yourself in this Alice-in-Wonderland kind of world, where you're so proud of yourself for somehow having set up three columns. Then all of a sudden you're in . . . *two* columns. Then you're in *one* column. Then the column's getting narrower and narrower and narrower, until there's this one column infinitely long and one character wide—and every time you hit ESCAPE it goes, HYPHEN, HYPHEN, HYPHEN, HYPHEN, HYPHEN, HYPHEN, HYPHEN, HYPHEN. . . . You turn off the computer, you turn it back on—IT'S STILL THERE!

So that's why, especially when working in columns, I need something soothing like letters. Just waiting for me in case I should start to lose my mind. I think those letters are what got me through the bills on Wednesday.

And when I got up on Thursday, I felt even a little better, so I got in a *half-hour* late. Now, fortunately, getting off the elevator with me when I arrived was this stocky Australian attorney from my floor. So as we walked past Marlina's desk, I walked on the exact opposite side of him, matching him step for step—using him as a moving pick, you see.

If it hadn't've been for those letters there waiting for me to mail them, I don't think I would have made it through Thursday. Because on Thursday I had to do *travel expense reports*. And travel expense reports, like bills, involve numbers and dollar signs and columns—but on top of that, there's the incredible emotional damage of seeing *what your boss spends on trips*.

It's extraordinary! Shelby had been to New York, my home-town, for a week. In that week, he had spent more than had been spent on my *childhood*. But what *really* got me was: unlike me, he didn't have to stay at my mom's.

If it hadn't've been for those letters, I don't think I would have made it through Thursday and those travel expense reports.

And when I got up on Friday, I felt about the same as I had on Thursday—so I got in a half-hour late again. I thought, "Hey, I'm the same amount late as Thursday. I've stanched the flow of blood!" I was so proud of myself, I didn't even think of being covert. I sauntered past Marlina's desk. "I'm just the same amount late! I'm just the same amount late!"

Marlina went, "Josh, can I have a word with you, please?"

"Uh . . . yes, Marlina?"

"Josh, why are you coming in so late?"

"Um, Marlina . . . Um . . . Personal problems. *Vague* personal problems."

"Well, Josh, are these personal problems going to continue?"

"Oh no, Marlina, they just cropped up this week for the very first time—a big anomaly in my life. After today, you'll see—I'll have no more personal problems."

"Well, Josh, I'm glad. . . . Now, please, don't think of me as an ogre. It's just that I'm the head secretary here. So if you're going to be late, please *call in* to me. If I'm not at my desk, leave me a message on my voice-mail. Okay?"

"Okay, Marlina. I will. But it'll never happen again. I'll never be late again."

I walked the lonely corridor, feeling an almost indescribable sadness. For I had just come to realize that Marlina did not love me unconditionally.

On Monday, I came in . . . an *hour* late. But I called in to Marlina's voice-mail, so I'm fine: "Uh, sorry—unanticipated extension of personal problems."

When I got in to work, the letters were still there in their pile, waiting to be mailed. But something had happened to them. They had lost their . . . glow. The magic was gone. It was like . . .

I don't know if you have ever, like, gone to a party and you start talking with someone—say, in my case, a woman—and you realize, right away: "We have nothing in common." And yet you think, "Perhaps if we keep talking together, we'll get to have sex with each other—and all those years I've spent *thinking* about sex will somehow have been worth it." And then you actually leave with her, and you go to her place, and you're kissing and hugging on her couch and you're thinking, "Wow, maybe we really *will* have sex together—and then we'll have that *orgasm* thing, and for a few seconds I won't have to think about death!" . . . And then you're naked with her in bed and—"AAH, AAH, . . . aah." . . . That was nice—and now this is . . . awkward. We don't know each other; we have nothing in common; and the buses have . . . *stopped.*

It wasn't that way with Helen. With Helen—after the first couple of weeks it takes me to loosen up in bed; after that—every little movement in bed, *every* little movement, was like . . . a communication. Every little movement, a communication. I think it's because we knew each other. Really knew each other. So every little movement, a communication. Because we knew each other. We *knew* each other.

Okay, now take these letters. Eighty-five or so communications I'm supposed to mail to eighty-five people I've never even *met??*

Fuck it.

By a week later, I was coming in to work consistently at least ninety minutes late every day. But I was calling in religiously to Marlina's voice-mail . . . so I'm fine. And at first I was leaving the same, generic message: you know, "Sorry—more personal problems, more personal problems . . ."

But around mid-week, something happened. I don't know what it was—maybe it was the early-morning quietude, maybe it was that time in my life—but I found myself starting to open up to Marlina's voice-mail. I started telling things to Marlina's voice-mail that I had not told anyone. Childhood traumas. Sexual fantasies—like the one where Dashiell Hammett hires me to be a sexual surrogate with Lillian Hellman and we rewrite her plays together. . . . You know, stuff I'm sure we've all *had,* but I'd never *shared* with anyone.

In that week, I felt I'd made more progress with Marlina's voice-mail than I had in *months* with my own therapist. And I think I understand why, too: my therapist, you know, I love her, and she's very bright—but I don't always get the sense that she's . . . *listening* to me. I never had that problem with Marlina's voice-mail. I always could tell that Marlina's voice-mail was listening to me. In fact, I could prove it. At the end of my message, I could press "1" and it would play the whole thing back to me, word for word. And then if I thought of something new while I was listening to myself, at the end I could press "6" and append *more* ideas. . . . Of course, this was making me much later for *work*—but I think that was easily compensated for by the fact that I was growing as a person . . . opening up emotionally . . . *Creatively,* too: I was getting what I thought was some really good writing done on my novel during work hours in my local directory.

In fact, when I came in that next Monday I was thinking about this chapter from my novel. I'd printed it out and wanted to work on it some more, but now the hard copy was lost under the huge mulch pile that inevitably forms on my desk because I never file anything. So I'm rooting around in this huge pile on my desk, looking for the chapter, when I happen to uncover . . . THE LETTERS—which I had totally forgotten about! It was like a slap of reality. I went, "SHIT! These letters are . . . LATE!"

What should I do? Should I put them in the OUT box? . . . No, no—too risky. What if they're still in the OUT box and Shelby happens to amble out of his office? "Hey, *that's* a lot of letters in my OUT box. I haven't mailed that many letters today. That's about eighty-five or so letters. . . . Wait—weren't those letters supposed to go out— Jo-o-ossshhh . . ."

"Ribbit. Ribbit. Ribbit. . . ."

No—I have to think of a better plan. . . . *I* know: I'll wait until Shelby gets on one of his incredibly long conference calls. Then, when he's on the call, I'll have all my envelopes lined up for maximum efficiency—and I'll seal the envelopes *really fast* and put them in the OUT box. If God is with me, the mail clerk will come and take them all away and mail them before the end of his call.

Okay—so I got all my envelopes lined up for maximum efficiency. And I had my tool to be efficient with: I had my inherited envelope moistener! I got my envelope moistener poised over the first envelope flap. It didn't take long—I could hear Shelby get a call in his office:

"Hello, Bill—yes, it's me. No, I'm not. Are you? Okay—so neither of us is touching anything. Now put Margaret on the horn. . . . Margaret, are you wearing your gloves? . . . Good. Let's get down to business, then. Nine hundred trillion! . . . Three hundred ninety-nine quadrillion! . . . Three point twelve infinity billion billion billion! . . ."

Time to get to work! I had my envelope moistener poised over the first envelope flap—when Ann Dickerson walked up. Ann Dickerson was Bob's "summer associate," and for those of you who may not know what a summer associate is: on the totem pole of power at a law firm, the summer associate is . . . under the ground. What they are, from what I've observed: they're law school students who spend the summer kissing ass and doing shitwork—and in return they get to be called "summer associates."

And of course there's a whole hierarchy of power at a law firm like S&M. The young attorneys are called "associates." And they're all like little frightened puppies: "Arf arf arf arf arf!" They're all frantically hunting for . . . billable rabbits.

Then you have your older, more successful attorneys: the partners. Now, don't get me wrong: they'll be running dogs their whole careers. Buy these guys, they're more like bigger, mangier dogs with spikes: "WOOF WOOF WOOF WOOF WOOF." They don't have to be so frantic, because they know where all the biggest, fattest billable rabbits are: "WOOF WOOF WOOF— Hello there, Jack!" CHOMP!

But summer associates—it's sad, really. Because they haven't even reached the *puppy* stage yet. They're more like a . . . pupa. All trying to poke their heads through the filament of their cocoons, and making their little pupa sound: "Voooo . . . voooo . . ."

Ann Dickerson was forever *just about* to deliver a litigation report to Bob (which is weird in itself, because Bob is not in litigation; I guess she wanted to impress him). But she was afraid of interrupting him while he was on an important call—which would be the end of her career and, thus, life. So Ann had this trick: she would watch the light of Bob's extension on my phone and wait for that light to go out, so then it would be safe for her to go in. But this trick would involve her having to mystically stare through my "wall"—past me, whom she never said hello to or acknowl-edged in any way—directly at the light of Bob's extension on my phone.

Which, under normal circumstances, *irritated* me—but on this particular occasion I was under a lot of *extra* time pressure, and having her go "Voooo . . . voooo . . ." right past me was throw-ing me off!

I thought, "Okay—I'm not going to let her throw me off; I'm not going to let her affect me. She doesn't know these letters are late. She doesn't even know I *exist*. I'm just going to go through with my plan, looking calm, cool, and professional."

So, looking calm, cool, and professional, I got my envelope moistener poised again over the first envelope flap, I ran it over the flap—but it didn't seal! I ran it over the envelope flap again—it still didn't seal. I felt the flap—*it was not moist.*

Okay. I didn't panic. I'd worked enough with these envelope-moistener things. I knew that sometimes they needed to be *coaxed*. Little, tiny squeezes. You want to coax that moisture all the way through the sponge tip, until that tip is fully engorged. Coax, coax, coax.

So, while still looking calm, cool, and professional, I coaxed my envelope moistener for a time. Then I went back and ran my moistener over the first envelope flap. It still didn't seal!

I felt the sponge tip. *It was as hard as a rock.* I had inherited a Paleolithic-period *artifact* of an envelope moistener! But now I had no other choice: I had to try to squeeze water *through* a stone. And as I was squeezing, I was thinking: "When that Ann

Dickerson gets out of her cocoon, she's gonna be SO FUCKING RICH!!!" And I squeezed really hard and the top flew off and all the water poured out and moistened all the letters and envelopes at once—along with the millions of Jujubes and Sugar Babies I keep around my desk to keep myself going during the day. They all mixed together into this organic *glop.* So, operating on pure instinct, I took everything off the top of my desk, threw it into a briefcase—and *I took an early lunch.*

Fortunately, they're already preparing Quarter Pounders with Cheese at 10:30 a.m., so I could have my usual nutritious meal. I went up to my favorite table—which I didn't have to fight anyone for because it's, you know, just 10:30. I sat down at the table and took stock of my situation.

As usual, I had begun to Fuck Up. Perhaps now, as usual, I should . . . QUIT! Yes, I can quit, and then I can call UNIFORCE and say, "Hello, it's me. I'm ready to go back into the field—so you can go back into operation. Just make sure you assign me to some nonsecretarial, non-legal, low-pressure word-processing gig—*please.*"

Like the one they sent me to once South of Market, at this engineering firm. I remember my first day, when I got introduced to the supervisor of word processors there: this tall, very elegant woman named Danielle. Very beautiful, very low key. *Very* low key. Comatose.

"Welcome, Josh—let me show you around. There's your desk, there's your phone, there's your pile of work, there's your computer. Okay, now that you've had the tour, let me share with you my philosophy of supervising: I'm Not Your Mother. So don't expect me to check when you come in to work, when you leave, when you go to lunch, when you come back from lunch, who you talk to on the phone, how long you talk. I don't care. Just do your work, we'll all be happy. Go ahead, bring in your Walkman, listen to your Walkman during the day. Just do your work, we'll all be happy. Now, is everything copacetic?"

"Uh . . . yes."

But it was better than that: I was *thrilled*. I had never *dreamed* I could listen to my Walkman while working at a day job downtown.

And my first couple of weeks at this job, I got to kind of live out this fantasy I'd always had. Because I always feel like I'm behind on news and events of the world. So my first couple of weeks at this job, I listened on my Walkman all day to National Public Radio. Till at the end of those weeks, I really felt as though I'd Considered All Things—you know, way more than I'd ever really wanted to.

So I started bringing in tapes and listening to tapes. And of course, you couldn't possibly listen to a Walkman while you were working as an actual secretary—because as an actual secretary, you do *this* task, which is interrupted by *this* task, which is interrupted by *this* task . . . But when you're a word processor, you just type—type, type, type, type type . . .

And it was even better at this job, because I didn't even have to juggle different projects. I was just typing my way through one project—one huge pile of work. At this engineering firm they design and build tunnels, and the project I was typing was all the engineering specs for this enormous tunnel they were going to build through a mountain on the island of Oahu, in Hawaii, connecting the towns of Haiku and Halawa. And as I typed my way through the massive Haiku Tunnel Project, I found out all the things that go into tunnels: the paint, the cement, the door-knobs . . .

Each day I would come in and work on my novel and type tunnel specs and listen to music on my Walkman and go to lunch and come back from lunch . . .

I was coming back from lunch one day when I happened to notice that Danielle was listening to her own Walkman. I said, "Danielle, what are you listening to?"

She said, "Oh, I'm just listening to myself."

I said, "What do you mean?"

She said, "Well, on the weekends, me and my girlfriends, we have a gospel singing group—and we made a demo tape, and that's what I'm listening to."

I said, "Oh, really—could I hear it?"

"Sure."

I put on her headphones:

"JESUS! WHOA—SAVE ME!! . . ."

My ears ringing, I handed the headphones back to her.

"Wow, Danielle, that's—that's very good! . . . You know, now that you've shared that side of yourself with me, I feel I can share *my* creative side with *you*. I'm a novelist."

"Oh. What have you written?"

"Uh . . . well, actually, I'm working on my first novel right now."

"Oh. When do you work on it?"

"Well, uh, . . . I can't work on it during the week, of course, because during the week I'm working *here*. And I *would* work on it on the weekends, but for some reason I can only write on a computer—and I can't afford a computer just yet. So I'm not, uh, actively working on it right now."

"Well, Josh. It must get boring typing tunnel specs all day. Why don't you take a couple of hours each day and work on . . . your novel?"

Oh . . . my . . . god.

I'm in *heaven!* . . . I'm getting *paid* to come in, listen to my Walkman, do some tunnel specs, and *work on my novel.*

And I was already in a great mood, because I had just split up with Helen—so I was in my initial post-Helen-euphoria period. It was like, "Ooh—I'm free! I can call up . . . Michelle Pfeiffer . . . Grace Paley . . . *anyone*—I'm free!!"

So I'd come in, listen to music, work on my novel, type some tunnel specs . . . No one knew my name. No one knew I existed. I was totally anonymous. I'd come late, go early. Go to lunch, come back from lunch. Talk on the phone, listen to music. No one knew I was there. No one knew I existed. I was a total *nobody* there. . . . And as the weeks went by, I found myself growing incredibly, incredibly . . . depressed.

And I couldn't understand why. It got to the point where I was so despondent one day, I had to call my incredibly smart best friend, Ed.

"Hi, Ed—I'm sorry to call you at work. I've just been having this terrible crisis here. I'm feeling so sad, and I don't know why. I mean, I have this great job, I'm free from Helen . . . Why am I so *sad?*"

He said, "Well, Josh—*think* about it, my friend. For the past month or so, you've been typing a *tunnel*. Right?"

"Yeah . . ."

"Well, Josh—has it occurred to you that, having typed a tunnel, you might now be finding yourself . . . *inside the tunnel?*"

He's right!!!

Having severed all my ties to earthly concerns, I now found myself in a place with no light, no contours, no end. *I was inside the Haiku Tunnel.* . . . And I never want to go back. I *never* want to go back.

But if I quit my job here at S&M, I'll go temp again and I'll be back in the Haiku Tunnel in no time—I just know it.

But how can I *not* quit my job here at S&M?

Okay, so I'm sitting at my table at McDonald's—next to me, a briefcase filled with glopped-together letters and Jujubes. Probably the Postmaster General will not accept them in that form. I think in order to save my job, I'm gonna have to mail out those letters. But in order to mail them out, it means I'm gonna have to . . . reconstitute them somehow. Which means I'd have to forge Bob's signature . . . (But that should be easy enough—it's pretty much a straight line.)

I realized that in order to save my job, I'd have to make the ultimate sacrifice: I'd have to come in and work on the weekend. So be it.

I came in late Saturday afternoon, went up to my desk, switched on the terminal, called up the document with the eighty-five or so letters, hit PRINT—and waited.

After a certain amount of time had elapsed, it occurred to me that it was taking far too long for the printer to begin printing out my letters. Far too long for the printer to begin eking out my eighty-five or so letters.

Oh, the printer must be out of paper!

So I went over to the printer—thinking that when I got there, the little readout window would tell me, "PAPER OUT"—and I would put some paper in the paper tray, and the printer would print me out my letters. But when I got to the printer, the little read-out window did not say, "PAPER OUT." It said, "PRINTER READY."

I said, "IF PRINTER 'READY,' WHY PRINTER NOT AL-READY 'PRINT'?!!! . . . JOSH LONG AGO 'READY'—THAT WHY JOSH HIT 'PRINT'!!! INTERVENING MUCH TIME ELAPSE, YET NOT EMERGE FROM PRINTER DESIRED LET-TERS!! 'PRINTER READY' NOT SUFFICIENT FOR JOSH. JOSH NEED MORE INFOR—"

Oh shit. *Oh shit.* Did I forget to initialize the printer?

Because if I did, you have to understand something: normally that central computer in Joliet leads a very boring existence—you know, 0-1-0-1. Very binary. But every once in a while some absent-minded person will forget to initialize his printer—and that's when the central computer gets to . . . let its hair down:

"Let's see. Where shall I print out those letters to cause young Joshua the *maximum* discomfort? Ha ha ha ha ha ha ha!"

I went into the printer directory going, "Please, just tell me you printed them out on my floor. *Please* tell me you printed them out on my floor." No! Not only did the printer directory tell me the computer had not printed out the letters on my *floor*—it told me the computer had printed them out in the other *building* that S&M has: the Pine Building, which—unlike *my* building, the Todd Building—is under heavy security at all times. . . . It even told me what *room* the letters were in: they'd been printed out in the printer in Room 1122 of the Pine Building.

Well, I don't know how I'm gonna get into Room 1122 of the Pine Building, but I'm gonna have to. Otherwise, I can just picture the scenario: on Monday morning, whoever works in Room 1122 of the Pine Building walks into his office. Finds, nestled in his printer, eighty-five or so letters. All marked "Personal and Confidential." All bearing the signature line of the feared Bob Shelby. . . . He quickly picks up the phone:

"Uh, hi, Mr. Shelby. You don't know me. I work over here in Room 1122 of the Pine Building. I have, oh, I'd say about eighty-five letters of yours here in my printer."

"Oh, really? Who are they addressed to?"

"Uh, they're addressed to . . ."

"Jo-o-ossshhh . . ."

"Ribbet. . . . Ribbet. . . . Ribbet. . . ."

Okay. I don't know how, but I need to retrieve those letters.

I went down to the street, and as I was walking the last block of Pine Street on my way to the Pine Building, I could feel myself changing—changing into something I recognized. It was the same feeling I'd had back in college, when on my way to my calculus final—not having attended *any* calculus classes since midterms. It's a feeling of, "I have been *fucking up.* And now *something* is about to happen. But I will *deal* with it—for I am . . . *Josh Kornbluth, Neurotic Adventurer!*"

I entered the massive doorway of the Pine Building—and as I walked up to the guard at his little guard desk, my thoughts became pellucid in their clarity. I stood looming over the guard at his guard desk.

I said, "Excuse me, I just printed out some documents—wrong printer, heh heh. I'll just go up and retrieve 'em and be right back down—"

"Do you have a pass?"

"Uh, no, I don't have a pass."

"Well, all attorneys have passes. Aren't you an attorney?"

"No, I'm not an attorney. I'm . . . JUST a secretary."

I have a problem with these people. I have a problem saying, "I'm a secretary." I always seem to end up saying, "I'm . . . JUST a secretary."

"Well, if you're JUST a secretary, then you need *authorization* to enter the Pine Building."

"Oh, really? Authorization from whom?"

"From an attorney, of course."

I said, "Wait. You're a guard. I'm a secretary. Together we cling to the bottom rung of the socio-economic ladder. Now you—a 'comrade,' if you will—you are telling me that before *you,* a 'comrade,' will let me in, that I have to get authorization from . . . an *attorney,* way up on the penthouse rung of the ladder?! You're saying that an *attorney* has to authorize *me* before *you,* a 'comrade,' will let me in??! . . . And what would 'authorize' *mean* to an attorney, anyhow? They just use language to lie and cheat and steal. To an attorney, 'authorize' could mean 'I piss on his grave'—not 'Let him into the building.' . . . YOU'RE SAYING *HE* HAS TO AUTHORIZE *ME* BEFORE *YOU* LET ME IN???"

"Yes."

"Okay."

So I came up with the names of about fifty attorneys I knew of at S&M.

Weird thing: early Saturday evening, none of them are in their offices.

Then I remembered: there's a *new* guy, a new young—you know, "Arf!"—associate. He works in my group, the Tax Group— been working there about a week. Likely to be working late on a Saturday, to impress everyone. Very friendly guy; always says hello to me in the morning. . . . There's just one problem: he hasn't quite gotten my *name* down yet. I mean, he's gotten the *J* part. But every morning, it's: "Helllooo, Joel!" . . . "Helllooo,

Jason!" . . . "Helllooo, Juan!" . . . I mean, he's closing in. He'll get there eventually.

I said, "Well, call this guy up and tell him it's '*Jesús.*' Maybe he'll think it's me."

He picked up the phone and dialed. . . .

"Hello, sir—I'm sorry to interrupt you. This is the guard at the Pine Building. I have a secretary here by the name of Josh Kornbluth. He seeks your authorization to enter the Pine Building. Will you grant such authorization?"

The guard put down the receiver. "He said, 'Okay.'"

I got my little temporary pass. As I was making my way towards the bank of elevators, all I could think of was, "If the hand of Fate has carried me this far—past the guard—perhaps Fate will also ensure that when I get up to Room 1122 of the Pine Building, it will turn out to be a room like . . . *my* 'room.' Not one of those rooms with actual walls and doors and locks that you can see and touch, or I might be up Shit Creek."

I was just about to get onto the elevator when the guard called after me, "Excuse me, don't you want the passkey that lets you into every office in the Pine Building?"

"YES!!!"

I took the passkey and went up to the— I don't know how to describe the 11th floor to you. It's . . . kind of slick, kind of plush. A lot of naugahyde, a lot of chrome. . . . It's the Criminal Division of S&M.

It's a good thing I had my passkey, because Room 1122 turned out to be one of those rooms with actual walls and doors and locks. It even had a name plate on the door: "J. A. FAUSTINO."

I knocked. *I hope he isn't here, whoever he is.* No answer. I tried my passkey. It worked! I pushed the door open, stepped inside, shut the door behind me, flipped on the light—and there, across a crowded little office, nestled in the top of a Hewlett Packard 2000BX Laser Jet printer, were my eighty-five or so letters!

I said, "I'm here! I'm here!"

I ran up and snatched them from their cradle and clutched them to my bosom.

"Oh, Josh, you've come for us!"

"Of course I have."

"But Josh, why did you print us out all the way over here?"

"Oh, you know *me*. . . . Shhhhhh. Shhhhhh. Shhhhhhhhhh."

And my letters and I were just about to make our getaway— when the doorknob jiggled, a key turned in the lock, the door opened . . . and in walked a young woman wearing spandex bicycle pants and a T-shirt.

At first, her attire threw me. I thought, "Who could this be?" Then I remembered: at these law firms they let their attorneys wear whatever they want on the weekends. That's why you can come in on a Sunday and see, like, a partner in a loincloth— hunting for boar with a crossbow. Because he *can;* it's allowed in the dress code.

I thought, "Oh! This woman must be J. A. Faustino!"

And she didn't freak out. Imagine that. She walks into her office Saturday evening and finds standing, trembling next to her printer, clutching documents, a strange (albeit cute) guy—and she didn't freak out. . . . I think I know why: she's in the Criminal Division, so she's used to dealing with criminals—which is evidently what I am.

I'm standing there clutching documents. I was about to say, "Letters!" But then I thought that might sound stupid. So I said, "Litigation report! Printed out on wrong printer! Sorry, gotta go!"

She didn't budge from the doorway.

She said, "Do you work in this building?"

"No, I work in the Todd Building—the *Todd* Building."

"The Todd Building, eh? And what *group* do you work in?"

Well, I remembered reading somewhere that when you're lying under intense pressure it's a really good idea to tell the truth as much as possible—so you don't cross yourself up with details. So I told her the truth. I said, "The Tax Group. I work in the Tax Group."

She said, "The Tax Group, eh?" And she began pacing in front of her doorway. "The Tax Group. It seems to me there's a very powerful partner who leads the Tax Group. I can't quite recall his . . . NAME."

Suddenly I felt like I was on the stand being cross-examined in one of those old *Perry Mason* episodes. I was waiting for that woman dressed all in black to leap up in the back of the courtroom and go, "*I* did it. Josh is innocent! He *tried* mailing the letters. I intercepted them—poured water on them—attached candies—it was *me!*" But this did not happen.

Fortunately, I had what I thought was the correct answer. I said, "You must be referring to the illustrious Bob Shelby."

I could see I was winning her over, so I added the icing to the cake: "You know, Bob Shelby and I work quite closely together."

She said, "Ooh! You work closely with Bob? May I . . . touch you?"

I said, "Well, all right. If only the hem of my . . . garment."

She said, "I can't believe this! Here it is, it's Saturday night, I'm coming back from my workout, and all I can think about as I walk down the hallway is, 'How will I ever solve this complicated tax problem I have with my own personal taxes?' . . . So now I walk into my office—and who should I find standing here by some quirk of fate, but some hotshot young attorney from the Tax Group. . . . Okay, Mr. Tax Hotshot—here's my complicated tax problem. . . ."

For the next fifteen or twenty minutes, she described to me—believe me!—a truly arcane and complicated set of tax problems. It involved . . . I think her parents had brought her burial plots in Liberty, Kansas, or something—and there were depreciations, loopholes . . . I couldn't follow it, of course.

And the whole time she was talking, I was homing in on her— on her— Well, to *me*, her . . . Helenosity. I think maybe it was the bicycle pants and the leg muscles and the freckles . . . I was kind of homing in on that when I heard her say, "So that's my complicated tax problem. Now, if you were in *my* position, what would *you* do?"

And I told her, truthfully: "I would not file."

She laughed and said, "No, *really.*"

So I went into my Escape Mode, where everything slo-o-ows down in my consciousness.

I said, "So-o-orrry, got to go-o-o now. Got to deliver this lit-iga-a-a-ation report. Maybe we could talk about this over lu-u-unch sometime."

And I don't know where she was keeping that big Filofax book in those pants of hers, but she pulled it out and said, "I'm al-ready boo-oo-ooked for lunch this week. Why don't we go out for drinks right no-o-ow?"

"Okay, uh, I'll meet you for drinks right after I drop this off."

"Where are you going?"

"Oh, I'm just taking this to my room. . . ."

"Wait! I'll come with you."

Oh, right—she's going to come with me . . . to my "room." She's going to be way fucking impressed: "Wow—you get a desk in the hallway? You're on your way to senior partner!"

I said, "No, I'm sorry—you can't come with me to my room."

"Why?"

"It's, uh—it's been . . . roped off. Yeah. Chemical spill. Lots of old coffee. . . . Tell you what: let's just meet in a half-hour at . . ." I went through my mental Rolodex of downtown places to meet: McDonald's—no. Burger King—no. Jack in the Box—*better,* but no. . . . Wait—*I* know! "Lascaux! I'll meet you in thirty minutes at Lascaux. See you there!"

And I wheeled around, and my letters and I were making our escape down the hallway, when she called out to me, "Hey, my name's Julie Faustino. What's yours?"

"It's Josh Kornbluth—" Oh, fuck!

I brought the letters back to my desk, put them back in their pile, covered them up. I'll deal with mailing them out during the week sometime. . . . Because right now I have this much more pressing matter to attend to: I have this attractive young woman waiting for me at Lascaux, expecting me to solve her complicated tax problem.

And I'll admit, my first instinct may have been to just *split*—maybe even leave the country. But I'd recently had a birthday, and on my birthday I had made this kind of silent vow to myself that I would try to begin living a moral life. (It's just a random quality I had picked out of the Talmud, but I wanted to stick to it.) I thought, "Well, the *moral* thing to do here is the *difficult* thing—and that is to go down there to Lascaux and tell her I'm not a tax attorney. And that's what I'm going to do!"

I went to Lascaux. As I was descending the stairs, I could see her sitting in a booth, all candlelit—she looked really nice.

Right when I sat down across from her in the booth, she leaned over and said, "Come on, Josh—'fess up, Mr. Tax Guy. What's your brilliant solution to my tax problem?"

I said, "Julie, I have to tell you something. I'm not a tax attorney. I'm not even an attorney. I'm . . . JUST a secretary. . . . And

I didn't mean to deceive you—really, I didn't. But when we met, up there in your office just now, you surprised me—and I have to admit, I was attracted to you; you reminded me of someone. And when I saw that you *assumed* I was an attorney, I couldn't bear to tell you I *wasn't*—and then see your eyes change. Change from looking-at-a-peer eyes to looking-down-at-me eyes. And I know that was wrong, and I think if you stick with me a little longer you'll see some nice compensating qualities. . . ."

That's what I *meant* to tell her.

No, really, I did! But right before I was about to say all that, there was this, like, chemical spill in my brain—it's a medical thing. It flooded the synapses, disconnecting the intention part, in the back of my brain, from the part that controls the mouth. So even as I was meaning to say all that, what actually came out of my mouth was, "Let's not talk about tax law right now, okay? In fact, let's not talk about tax, or law, or anything with 'law' in it. Like *in-law*. Or *lawn*."

She said, "Josh, I'm sorry. Where are my manners? You've probably been working—what?—seventy or eighty hours this week on tax problems. You come down here on a Saturday night—and what do I do but hit you with yet another tax problem. I'm sorry, Josh—like you, I'm burnt out; my manners are shot. *Please* allow me, by way of apology, to buy us both drinks."

"Okay."

I don't know what it is about Crystal Geyser, but it opens me right up. Did the same for her. We started sharing our life stories. She told me about her parents: her father, a district court judge in

Maryland; her mother, an architect. A very low-powered family. . . . I, in turn, told her about my own illustrious family, of unemployed Stalinists and Trotskyites in New York.

She was laughing. I said, "Why are you laughing?"

She said, "Josh, with that family background—and loving your parents as you obviously do—how did you ever decide to become a *corporate attorney?*"

"That's a good question, Julie. A very good question. . . . Okay, I'll tell you.

"Back in college, me and my first true love, my first girlfriend, uh, Lisa Gibson—we were very much in love, but very different. Lisa was going to be a lawyer; she was going to go to law school. I was going to be a novelist; I was a creative writing major. Very different, but very much in love. . . .

"Then, right before the end of the school year, Lisa Gibson was, uh, crossing the street when she was, like, *hit by a truck and killed.* And I decided that if I, you know, truly loved her, I should follow in her karmic footsteps (if you will) and attend law school in her place. . . .

"And then, when I actually got into law school, I thought that if I *truly* loved her, I couldn't just support my *own* family, I should support *her* family as well—so I couldn't become one of those nice attorneys who help poor people and immigrants; I had to become a big, rapacious corporate attorney. And that's what I did."

She said, "Josh, that's an *incredible* story. And tell me, where did you go to law school?"

Okay. What places have law schools? Um . . . New York University. Yeah! N.Y.U. . . .

"N.Y.U.! I went to N.Y.U. Law School."

"Oh, really? Then did you ever take a class there with Professor James Mankowski?"

Now, here's the weird part . . . I had! When I was ten or eleven—maybe twelve—me and my mom would trundle downtown to the New School for Social Research, in Greenwich Village. We took a class there with a guy named Professor James Mankowski!!

I said, "Oh, you mean a little guy with a pipe and his hair all swirling around?"

She said, "Yeah, that's him."

I said, "Oh, he's a wonderful professor! He's brilliant!" I didn't tell her it was a class in *yoga.*

She said, "Josh, Professor James Mankowski is my . . . *god-father.*"

I thought, "WHAT is going ON here??? The LIES . . . are mixing with the TRUTHS . . . to form some potent new REALITY. . . ." For a second I thought, "WAIT, maybe I *am* a tax attorney!!! Yes! And then I must be making a lot of *money,* and it's gotta *be* somewhere, and I'm gonna *find* it!"

And she was looking at me with such joy, such respect . . .

She said, "Josh, what you did was so loving, so giving. But I must confess . . . it also makes me sad, for you gave up your dream—your dream of becoming a novelist."

I said, "Julie, you can dry your eyes. I'll let you in on a little secret: you know when we just met, up in your office, and I was retrieving that 'litigation report'? It wasn't a litigation report—it was the last chapter of my *novel*. Knopf was waiting for it, and I just happened to print it out on the wrong—"

"Josh! You work eighty, ninety, perhaps a hundred hours a week as a tax attorney—*and* you're completing a novel for a major publishing house? *You* lead a double life!"

I said, "Julie, *you* don't know the half of it."

And when I woke up on Monday morning, I was *filled* with vim and vigor. I *leapt* out of bed. I *ran* into the shower. I *leapt* out of the shower—which I know is dangerous; I was just feeling that way.

I was running *early*. Even so, I really felt I needed to call in to Marlina's voice-mail. I had just gotten so used to sharing with Marlina's voice-mail all my deepest, most intimate experiences— like the one I'd just had with Julie Faustino at Lascaux.

And when I got in to work . . . Well, you have to understand something: after the very first of my hundreds of taped confessions to Marlina's voice-mail—after the *very first one*, Marlina never so much as looked *up* when I walked in. It was great.

But on this particular day, I was walking past Marlina's desk when she said, "JOSH, YOU *MUST* TELL HER."

"Okay, Marlina—I'll tell her. I'm going to my desk right now and I'm gonna tell her."

I picked up my phone and began dialing. But I have this

problem whenever I have to make a really difficult call: right before the last digit, I hang up. I try again—and right before the last digit, I hang up. It's an involuntary reflex. 1, 2, 3, 4, 5, 6—HANG UP! 1, 2, 3, 4, 5, 6—HANG UP! . . . It's especially hard to do with the internal four-digit extensions at S&M: 1, 2, 3—HANG UP! You have to be really fast. 1, 2, 3—HANG UP! 1, 2, 3—HANG UP!

And I think I was just about to summon the self-control necessary to dial all four of Julie Faustino's digits, get through to her, and tell her I wasn't really a tax attorney—I think I was *just about* to do that . . . when Shelby's door popped open, his head popped out, and he went: "JOSH, COME IN HERE!!!"

He had never *barked* at me before!

As I entered Shelby's office, I realized I didn't know where precisely to focus my terror. Should it be on . . . the letters? You'd think after a month and a half goes by and eighty-five important letters haven't gone out, that would start to filter back to him somehow. . . . Or did he hear about me impersonating an attorney with Julie? . . .

"So Josh. I know what you're going to think. You're going to think there's a double standard here, at S&M, between attorneys and secretaries. And you know something, Josh? You'll be right. But it's just the way it is. So I must insist that, as my secretary, . . . you keep your desk neat and clean at all times."

"Uh . . . sir, is that . . . *it?*"

"Look, I *know* it's a double standard, Josh. *My* office is often quite messy. But as a secretary, you *must* keep your desk neat and clean at all times."

"Sir! I'll be *happy* to clean off my desk! Thank you for *only* wanting me to clean off my desk. Look! I'm going to clean up my desk right now!"

I went out to my desk. *Wait! I can't clean off my desk. If I start to clean off my desk, I'll expose the letters, and he might see the letters. SHIT!!*

I ran to Marlina's desk.

"Marlina! I— Yes, I was just *about* to call Julie and tell her I wasn't really a tax attorney. But then Shelby's door popped open, his head popped out—he said, 'JOSH, COME IN HERE!!!' He says I have to clean off my desk *right away.* WHAT DO I DO???"

She said, "Well, Josh, why don't you take everything off the *top* of your desk, put it in *boxes,* and put the boxes *under* your desk?"

"Hmm. . . . Good idea—thanks!"

I went to the Xerox room, got a couple of empty boxes, brought them back to my desk, started shoveling everything *really fast* off the top of my desk into the boxes. . . .

Now, a few years back, I'd worked at my first secretarial job—at Caltech, the California Institute of Technology. A nice, friendly, homey little place to work. I was the assistant to the head secretary of the Physics Department. One week my boss, Milla Gilman, the head secretary, went away on vacation—leaving me to do all the things *she* normally did. The biggest task of which was to forward the voluminous mail that came in to former students and professors in the Physics Department: most of whom were from other countries—countries that use languages and alphabets *far* different from our own.

Milla Gilman, having been there forever, and being a super-secretary—she would just cross out the old address, write in the new one in Sanskrit, and mail it out. . . . I, however, did not have those resources. I thought, "Jeez, will I have to call the Mormons and get genealogical charts?!"

Well, it's just Monday. I'll just leave all this unforwarded mail in a pile on my desk.

Tuesday came around. *Well, it's just Tuesday. I'll just add this unforwarded mail to the pile on my desk.*

By Friday, I had this *huge* pile of unforwarded mail on my desk. I realized I couldn't possibly make a dent in that pile before Milla came back on Monday. So, not knowing what else to do, I took all the unforwarded mail and put it in a couple of boxes—and I put those boxes in a closet off the corridor. And I covered those boxes with my underwear.

I don't think I've mentioned that I was *living* in that closet at the time. I mean, technically I did have an apartment, but I was kind of way behind on the rent, and my roommates were kind of big and strong. So it was just a lot healthier and safer for me to live in that closet at Caltech. And my—I thought—brilliant idea of leaving my underwear on top of the boxes was that if Milla should happen to walk into the closet, she'd see . . . the underwear: "Hey, Josh—underwear!" She wouldn't think of looking *under* the underwear, seeing the true crime. . . .

As the weeks went by, I realized there was no way I could possibly forward those letters without getting Milla's help. But in order for me to get Milla's help, I'd have had to confess that I had not forwarded the letters when I was supposed to forward them—and I couldn't really see confessing that to Milla.

Each night I would sleep on the cold stone floor in the closet, next to the boxes, the telltale letters pulsating in my conscience.

Finally, I just couldn't take it anymore. I called up my friend JoJo, who had a car.

I said, "JoJo, there's no moon tonight. Pick me up at midnight outside Caltech." At midnight, JoJo pulled up. I brought out the boxes of letters. He drove me across town. And I threw out *all the unforwarded mail* . . . into a dumpster.

And you know, it was weird. I couldn't read a lot of the letters—because, you know, they were in different languages. But you could always somehow get the gist by looking at the handwriting through the crinkly thin blue aerogram paper. The letters said things like: "Your sister just had a baby." Or: "Your dog died."

And as I threw out those items of mail one at a time, I had this unanticipated sensation: I felt as though I was the ultimate fiction writer! It was like: "Your sister hasn't had a baby yet." . . . "Rover's fine!" . . .

I can't leave Shelby's letters in these boxes! If there's *one* thing

I've learned in my secretarial career, it's that when I put mail in boxes, it never, *ever* will go out.

I've got to quit. Even though I know that means I'll have to go temp again and I'll be back in the Haiku Tunnel in no time. I don't see any other way out.

So I typed a resignation letter. It wasn't any great literary masterpiece: "Dear Bob: I quit. Josh."

I printed out my resignation letter, put it in an envelope, left the envelope in his IN box, and went to lunch.

When I came back from lunch, his IN box was empty. So he'd probably read my resignation letter. But he was no longer in his office. So I had to sit at my desk, and wait for him to return and respond.

I sat there, hunched over my computer keyboard—typing, I think, the alphabet, over and over—listening for footsteps down the hallway.

I heard footsteps! NO-O-O-O-O!

I looked up. The *last* person I expected to see standing before me: Julie A. Faustino! Now wearing her full, during-the-week lawyer regalia.

She said, "Oh hi, Josh. I was just in the neighborhood, and I thought I'd— Oh, so *this is* your 'room'— Uh, gotta go." And she was gone.

I thought, "Great. I was just *about* to call her. Perhaps if I'd gotten through to her first and explained about this little misunderstanding about me being a tax attorney . . . maybe then we could have had a life together. But now she found out before I

could tell her, so to her I'm just the lying scum of Earth. . . .
Nothing really left for me to do but go back to typing the alphabet, listening for footsteps. . . ."

I heard footsteps! NO-O-O-O-O!

It was Shelby! Walking straight towards me, with this little
glint in his eye and this little demonic smile on his face, he said,
"Hey, *there* he is!" . . . walked right past me and into his office.

How he knew to say that phrase to me at that moment, I'll
never know. "Hey, *there* he is!" He'd never said it to me before
then. He's never said it to me since. "Hey, *there* he is!" How
Shelby could have possibly known that that was the exact expression my *father* used to say to me, when we hadn't seen each other
in a while. "Hey, *there* he is!" How Shelby could somehow have
intuited that this would make me feel like I was about to resign
from my *dad,* I don't know.

He's in his office. The door is shut. Is anything ever going to
happen?

Presently, his door opened a crack. His head slid out.

"Uh, Josh?" He beckoned.

I walked the gangplank onto the scaffold, hoping that in his
kindness the executioner would allow me to pick the kind of rope
I'd be hanged with. Like maybe, instead of an instant-death rope,
I'd get a two-week's-notice rope—or a rope where you get medical benefits for another couple of months afterward. . . .

"So Josh. I read your letter. What seems to be the problem?"

"Bob. Sir. I'm a bad secretary. I'm a *really* bad secretary.

Like, a lot of times when you see me on the phone, I'm not talking to clients—I'm talking to my friends. And other times, when you see me typing, I'm often not working on your memos—I'm working on my own novel and putting it in my local directory. . . . I'm bad, sir. I'm *bad*. I haven't even m—— the I——— . . . I haven't m—— the— I'm *bad*. Okay, sir? I'm BAD!"

"Josh, are you telling me that you're . . . behind?"

"I'm *evil*, okay? *Ich bin ein* evil secretary! I'm a bad seed. You want to get me out of the Tax Group, or I'll infect the other secretaries—you know I will! You'll see: they'll be talking on the phone with my friends, and typing my novel into their local directories. . . . I'm *evil*. I'm—*I'm attracted to your daughter in the picture!* I'M EEEEEEEEVIL!!!"

"Josh, you know what I think your problem is? I think you just have an artistic temperament. Now, this is what I think you're going to do. You're going to go back to your desk, settle down, focus, . . . and catch up."

I stared at him.

He said, "Go back to your desk, settle down, focus, . . . and catch up."

I said, "Sir, are you saying that you're not letting me . . . *quit?*"

"Go back to your desk. Settle down. Focus. And catch up."

"Yes, sir, I will."

I went back to my desk, sat down, and considered this unprecedented turn of events. As usual, I had fucked up. But now it was looking like, for the first time ever in my secretarial career, when the shit would finally hit the fan, *I'd still be around to be splattered by it.*

This was a *true* emergency! I had to call my incredibly smart best friend, Ed.

"Hi, Ed—it's me. I'm sorry to call you at work. It's just that I'm having a terrible crisis here. You know those letters I never mailed out? . . . Right, *those* letters. Well, I decided I'm never gonna mail them. . . . Right! I'm never gonna mail them. So I quit! . . . Right! I wrote a resignation letter. I brought it in to Shelby. AND HE WON'T LET ME QUIT! I'M STILL WORKING HERE! One day he's gonna find out I never mailed out those letters. He's gonna go, 'Jo-o-o-ssshhh . . .' and turn me into something! WHAT DO I DO???"

"Well, Josh, back up a second here. Now, did you just say that you just . . . *quit?*"

"Yeah."

"And yet, you're still . . . *working* there?"

"Right."

"Well, Josh, correct me if I'm wrong here—but I don't think you have anything to worry about. I mean, YOU'VE ALREADY QUIT. What *more* can they *do* to you?"

He's right!!

I've already quit! I voluntarily went up onto the scaffold and allowed myself to be hanged. . . . And yet, *I'm still here.*

I must now be in some new phase. I must now be one of the un-dead. Or perhaps the un-fired.

I looked under my desk—there were the boxes. I pulled off the tops—there were the letters. No longer did the letters say to me "comfort." No longer did they say "sex" or "guilt." They were just . . . *letters.*

I took them out of their boxes, put them on the desk in front of me, began sealing them and putting them in the OUT box. I didn't feel depressed anymore. I didn't feel anxious. I didn't feel wildly hopeful of artistic success. I just felt . . . *normal.*

Marlina D'Amore walked by. "How's it going, Josh?" she said.

"Oh, I'm just mailing out some letters."

She said, "I'm glad."

afterword

I can't tell you how weird it is for me to see these monologues in print.

For a couple of reasons. One, I never wrote them down when I performed them—I memorized them and recited them pretty much word-for-word (I have very few other skills, by the way). Two, this miraculous career as a monologuist, which coalesced from the chaos of my late twenties and early thirties, probably would never have happened if I hadn't suffered from terrible writer's block. (I know "terrible writer's block" sounds redundant: what writer's block *isn't* terrible? But ask anyone who worked with me at the *Boston Phoenix*—my block was bigger than their block.) It was so hard for me to set words down on a page (or screen) that I essentially had to give up being a journalist.

At least, give up being a *writing* journalist. I could still copy-edit. In fact, that may have been part of my problem—that my first paying job was not as a reporter or critic, but as a copy editor. The anal side of me—which I attribute to my mom, a cataloguing librarian and a Stalinist (talk about systems!)—was developed too soon . . . perhaps like the young pitching prospect who's mistakenly encouraged to develop a screwball before his arm has fully matured. I got so used to being rewarded for squeezing the errors out of other people's writing, it became impossible for me not to attack my own. Attack viciously—sentence by sentence. I would spend hours and hours rewriting and *re*-rewriting my lead—printing each one out before deleting it, in case I realized down the road that the one I'd written six hours ago was the correct, the perfect, the only sentence that could launch a review of, say, *The Alan Thicke Variety Hour.*

So I gave up writing. But in my own particular way: I told myself I *wasn't* giving up writing, and then proceeded not to write anything. For a while, I tried throwing myself into my copyediting, but I'd always wanted to be some sort of swashbuckler, and I found it real hard to swashbuckle as a copy editor.

Then the editor of the Arts section—a fantastic, careful editor, *creatively* anal—left the *Phoenix* for greener pastures (not hard to do, considering what a cheap bastard the publisher was). And my *Phoenix* writer-friends Scott Rosenberg and Owen Gleiberman (assiduous deadline-meeters both, damn them!) and I wrote a little sketch, which we performed at the Arts editor's going-away party at the HooDoo Barbecue in Kenmore Square. This was the first time I had performed in anything since I'd played the Third Shepherd in *The Second Shepherd's Play* in fifth grade at Cathedral School. (And I was *better* than James Blount, who got to star as the Second Shepherd; Mr. Pearlstine was playing favorites—again.) Our *Phoenix* sketch went over well (though the scummy publisher made a point of telling me, cruelly but wisely, "Don't give up your day job")—and I had a distinct sensation: *This is more gratifying than copyediting.*

And yet, seriously considering becoming a performer didn't occur to me until a couple of years later. By that point, I'd seen my own newspaper, the *Kenmore Comet,* fold after all of five bi-weekly issues—so much for my being the second coming of I. F. Stone. After putting the *Comet* to bed for the last time, I went on a long walk with Scott. I told him I didn't know what to do with my life. He asked me what I *wanted* to do. The question somehow took me off guard, but not as much as my answer: A comedian, I told him—*that's* what I wanted to be.

The strange thing is, I never went to comedy clubs. One of the few times I'd seen a comedian perform live—a comedienne, actually—was when I was in college and I saw Elayne Boosler open up for (I think) the Roches at the Bottom Line one summer. I couldn't believe that someone would actually come out on stage and tell jokes to strangers; it seemed just too bizarre and kamikazelike. The idea that I—the least physical person I knew, a copy editor for Christ's sake!—would one day blurt out to a dear friend that I wanted to do such a thing . . . Preposterous.

But Scott said, "Well, why don't you try it, then?" So I did.

I signed up for Open Mike Night at a comedy club called Stitches. (You gotta love those comedy-club names.) Right before I went on, I scribbled down two "political" jokes: one about President Reagan wanting détente with the Kremlin because he heard they had a Polyp Bureau; the other about his recent urological surgery being the inspiration for trickle-down economics. (Hey! I was new at this.) I went up on stage and told my two jokes and nobody laughed, except for Scott and Owen. I said some other things that occurred to me until my five minutes were up, at which point I left the stage to a smattering of grateful applause. As I made my way back to the table where my friends were sitting, some crewcut guy slapped me on the back and said something like: "Don't feel bad, fella!" Which was sweet of him. But the thing is, *I felt great!* I'd *loved* being on stage, in the beautiful spotlight—with the dust and smoke sifting through it, with the dim faces below staring up at me. Not that I ever wanted to set foot in a comedy club again, unless Richard Pryor or Woody Allen was playing there—but what a thrill to perform! Making up stuff as an audience of strangers watched me, *I didn't edit myself: I riffed.*

But if not in comedy clubs, then where? Taking a cue from Garrison Keillor's *A Prairie Home Companion*, I did my own such program for a year: I called it *The Urban Happiness Radio Hour.* It debuted at the HooDoo Barbecue, and as far as I know only three or four people ever heard it. We were broadcast out of an ancient "community" radio station, our engineer was perpetually stoned, and I think the station's signal was on the tentative side. And no one got paid. The best part, for me, was hanging out with Scott, whom I enlisted to play "Fred Schmertz," an enormously bitter film critic for whom every movie was a cruel reminder of some failed relationship. After each show, I'd wake the engineer to say good-bye, and then Scott and I (and eventually Ed Wells, a piano player and arranger I'd met in tap-dance class—don't ask; my foot still hurts) would go out to some Harvard Square café— and I'd look around in awe at all the fascinating people who were totally unaware that we'd just done a live radio show. It was kind of like *negative* fame, and it had its own perverse thrill.

And then, after a year, *Urban Happiness* disintegrated. Something about having no money and no audience did it in, I think. And here again my Scott Rosenberg–as–savior theme recurs. Just after the end of *Happiness* he took me along to see a monologuist named Spalding Gray, who was performing a retrospective of his work at the Brattle Theater in Cambridge. I had no idea that there *was* such a thing as a "monologuist"—as opposed to, say, a stand-up comedian, or the Homer of antiquity. We sat down in comfy chairs in a lovely theater (much nicer aesthetically than either Stitches or the HooDoo) and watched Gray sit at a desk and perform *Sex and Death to the Age 14.*

I don't know which thrilled me more: the exquisite, tender story Gray told, or the exquisite, tender, appreciative audience who surrounded me. That there *was* such a forum for the exchange of whimsy and irony and love stories of regret filled me with a racing, tremulous kind of hope that I hadn't felt since . . . well, since before my father, Paul, had gotten seriously ill and then died, three years earlier. Perhaps in a way Gray's tales (I saw several other pieces of his during that run) reminded me of the way my dad used to tell stories about himself—stories mostly, in Dad's case, about getting fired from jobs, about failed relationships, and always, always about the evils of the class system. Stories, no matter how ostensibly grim their subject, that were told with such *joy* that as a child I was convinced there was nothing more romantic than fucking up. (I was mistaken—wasn't I?)

Reflecting on Gray's work, I realized what a large part of my soul was filled with my father's stories—stories told by my father and also, even before his own lips were stilled, stories I told about him. I remember saying to some woman, around that time, that my father was the most interesting thing about me, and her telling me that that was a sad thing to say, and me thinking her wrong as could be. I guess, looking back on it, that I set out to prove my point somehow.

I wangled a thirty-minute gig out of the owners of a Cambridge restaurant-nightclub called "TT the Bear's Place"—who, perhaps because I'd eaten so much of their blackened catfish and drunk so much of their Diet Coke, felt they owed me the opportunity. I arranged to go up on stage between acoustic sets by a band called Scruffy the Cat. My plan was to talk about what my dad had told me about sex—stuff like him nicknaming me "Little Fucker," and other details that have had me defending him to my therapists ever since. First I tried to write a script—but I had even less success meeting my own deadline than I'd had with my editors' at the *Phoenix*. Then I read in Gray's introduction to one of his books that he didn't work from a script. Aha! I put key phrases down on index cards and, on the three nights leading up to my gig at TT the Bear's, I went to Scott's apartment and practiced riffing off those cards.

I learned a couple of things right away. The first thing I learned was that if I went through all the eighty-five or so index cards I'd prepared, my performance would last longer than the *Mahabharata*. The second thing I learned—or had my suspicions confirmed about—was that perhaps having no training whatsoever as a stage performer could be a liability in the monologuing field. You know your stagecraft is primitive when you're practicing for a solo performance and you keep upstaging yourself.

Nonetheless, I showed up at TT's on the appointed night, and I went up on stage and riffed my way through six or seven key phrases like "Little Fucker" and "Two Holes" and "Lubrication." Scott was there. Owen was there. Ed was there. And they weren't the only ones who laughed—though few laughed as enthusiastically, I'll admit. I was scared blind—and yet, I loved it. Loved it more than anything I'd done. More than telling bad jokes at Stitches. More than copyediting. And I didn't have to write stuff down: to meet my deadline, all I had to do was step on stage and open my mouth!

A guy named Oliver Platt (now a ubiquitous, rubber-faced movie actor) came up to me after my set. Raising his voice to be heard over the sounds of Scruffy, he said he didn't understand why more people hadn't laughed at my stories (a comment that somehow had the effect of endearing him to me). Then he told me he was involved with a new comedy revue called "The Gramm-Rudman Act" and invited me to their upcoming auditions. I went, brought Ed along with me to play the piano (giving my material the illusion of professionalism), and sang some original compositions—the one I remember the best being a set-to-music transcription of several saucy "Personals" ads from the *Phoenix*. And thus I became a professional performer—if $30 prorated over five months counts as professional.

During the run of "Gramm-Rudman," I kept trying to perform a little piece about going walking with my dad. But at the weekly tryouts for new sketches, the producer—a man who wore sandals and the sad expression of one who missed the crystalline asceticism of grad school—always found my story to be lacking a . . . point. (*I* knew the point: the point was that I wanted to tell it.) So I kept singing my little songs—and in the meantime performing at . . . Open Mike Nights.

I mean, I *wanted* to try developing my autobiographical monologue—but the more theater I saw, the more intimidated I was by my own lack of experience. Spalding Gray, Lily Tomlin, Eric Bogosian—these were stage artists with tremendous and varied training. My training, if any, was in correcting "theatre" to "theater" as called for by Associated Press style. So instead I aimed low: I developed my little five-minute stand-up set, and I performed it for mostly baffled audiences in Boston. Then I moved to San Francisco (at the invitation of Scott, who'd been recruited by fellow *Phoenix*-ites Michael Sragow and Glenda Hobbs to review plays for the *Examiner*) and performed the same five-minute set for mostly baffled Bay Area audiences.

Well, the weather was nicer.

But spending time in comedy clubs still made me cringe (except for when I got the chance to see a genius comic like Paula Poundstone at the Other Café, in the Haight). I didn't want to reduce my heritage to short sets with superficial jokes; I wanted to do long sets—*really* long sets. And I wanted to tell my stories in an environment that afforded the teller the aesthetic freedom granted, say, a poet at a reading. Not in a theater, though—not at first—because that was too scary.

The opportunity came via the celebrated satirist Charlie Varon, an old friend of . . . Scott's. (Are you sensing any sort of pattern?) Charlie knew I dreamed of monologuing, and one day he asked if I wanted to share an afternoon of trying out material at the Modern Times Bookstore. Trepidatiously, I accepted—and, surrounded by Charlie's smiling fans, family, and friends (to whom my Communist Jewish background was not, let us say, alien), I riffed about my dad and my mom and their friends. And it felt good. Although for months afterward I continued to pursue my stand-up "career" (moving laterally along the gutter of the industry), I kept on the lookout for another, Modern Times–like opportunity to try monologuing again. So that when a space opened up at a short-lived basement nightclub in North Beach called "Enrico Banducci's hungry id," I took a chance and did my first run there—a continually developing, improvised piece about my radical upbringing that I called *Josh Kornbluth's Daily World*.

Through the kindness of a friendly theater-booker named Evy Warshawsky, *Daily World* was soon able to move from the hungry id to a legitimate theatrical venue: the New Performance Gallery. And for the first time, I got reviewed. Now some people besides my friends started showing up. The monologue ended up running for six months at various San Francisco venues—not always *large* venues, mind you, but still . . . Suddenly I was a monologuist. I had a full-length piece, I had reviews, and (*pace* the *Phoenix*'s sleazy but canny publisher) I still had my day job.

Which for several years had been temping as a secretary, especially at law firms. So when I was invited to create a second monologue for a new festival called Solo Mio, I made that the subject of my next piece, *Haiku Tunnel*. I was desperate to see whether I could tell a story that didn't depend on the colorful characters in and around my family. The show turned out to be a lot of fun, and my boss (to my indescribable relief) an excellent sport about having been the unwitting model for "Bob Shelby," ultra-scary tax lawyer. *Haiku* also marked my discovery of the joys of collaboration—here with a director named David Ford, who helped me shape my improvs and (equally important) bribed me out of lethargy with promises of delicious cocoa and healthy sandwiches. Now I could spend countless hours investigating blind alleys with a collaborator, and then present the fruits of those labors at various theatrical venues—especially the Marsh, a magical "breeding ground" run by Stephanie Weisman, which has given so many of us monologuing weirdos a safe place to try anything in front of adventurous audiences.

The next year I collaborated with my younger brother Jacob and an actor-writer named John Bellucci (guess who introduced us—okay, I'll tell you: Scott) on a piece called *The Moisture Seekers*—which originally was going to be about a psychosomatic ailment, but then so many people said, "Moisture Seekers! Ha ha. A piece about sex!" that I gave in and made it a piece about sex.

Communism . . . secretarial work . . . sex. Without my planning it, somehow my topics were getting progressively more— shall I say, "accessible"? Enough Bay Area theater-goers were able to relate to the seeking of moisture that I finally felt ready to quit my day job.

Almost instantly, I got a call from Erin Sanders, dramaturg at an Off-Broadway theater called the Second Stage, inviting me to combine *Daily World* (Communism) and *Moisture* (sex) into a piece called *Red Diaper Baby* and bring it all back home to the Upper West Side, the land of H&H Bagels and Zabar's.

On the first preview night, my mom, Bunny, sat in the front row and laughed really loudly—which I found somewhat intimidating: I mean, would Lenny Bruce's mom have done the same? (Probably.) My tiny Maoist stage manager, Buzz Cohen, the playful but somewhat prudish daughter of Jewish Republicans, said after the show that a key episode in the piece, "Marcie's orgasm" (which Buzz could never bring herself to watch but always timed on her stopwatch), had . . . for some reason . . . run dangerously short. Carole Rothman and Robyn Goodman, Second Stage's gorgeous and brainy co-producers, sprang into action—promptly calling my mom and lying that her reservations for press night had to be canceled as a result of overbooking.

(Mom *was* allowed to several performances *after* press night, of course. One of my great pleasures was in overhearing her answers to strangers' questions about the truth of my stories. Once, I heard someone ask her whether she'd really served me double-espressos starting when I was four. Totally innocently, Mom responded, "Well, yes—but I only ran them through the filter *once.*")

The run (which continued down in Greenwich Village, at the Actors' Playhouse) was a joy—especially as I got to spend rehearsals listening to the zany stories of my director, Josh Mostel, who also knew a thing or two about growing up in the shadow of a charismatic radical Jewish father. (And who nearly brought me to tears with the most amazing opening-night gift: an original drawing by his dad, Zero.)

Coming back to San Francisco, and faced with the pressure to create a new monologue for the next Solo Mio fest, I returned to another of the passions that—along with Communism and a general lasciviousness—my father had tried passing on to me: math. Revisiting the site of my most monumental academic failure (and that's saying something), I hit the calculus books again until—just as I had freshman year at Princeton—I "hit the wall." It was tricky trying to figure out how to weave the (fictionalized) autobiography with the (real) math—though I realized, to my simultaneous joy and horror, that *The Mathematics of Change* would force me for the first time to have a theatrical "set": a rather large blackboard that immediately put audiences in a state of chalky, Pavlovian terror. I worked with John Bellucci on this piece for months: we shuttled back and forth between Los Angeles (his home) and San Francisco (mine). Our collaboration on *Math* is probably my favorite creative experience to date. It was nuts, though! Getting the story right, getting the math right (you wouldn't believe how many theater-goers know calculus—and aren't afraid of demanding corrections), getting the chalk not to squeak . . . But when it was done, and I was able to unwind a bit at the opening-night buffet put together by Solo Mio's ultraphotogenic producers, Joegh Bullock and Marcia Crosby, it struck me that again I had—with lots of help—been able to rekindle a proximity with my late father that would normally be denied a God- and Heaven-doubter like me.

At least, that's what I think about most in relation to these monologues: my dad, I mean. I miss him. I also miss my stepmother, Sue (who, though nineteen years younger than Dad, followed him to the grave not long after), a stubborn and playful woman who created an aura of Midwestern, down-to-basics innocence while seeing *everything*. And yet . . . I still have my wonderful girlfriend, Sara Sato. I have my amazing siblings, Jacob, Amy, and Sam. There's my mother, now a born-again macrobioticist who—when I visit—dilutes my coffee with decaf. My grandpa Julius, still singing and making jokes at 102 (he wants to know when I'll pay his "commission" for his bedtime story I retell in *Red Diaper Baby*). And—oh!—friends, such warm friends. Scott Rosenberg fell in love with a beautiful woman named Dayna Macy and married her (but it's okay, because he's not reviewing plays anymore, so I'm not missing out on any comps). John, and Mike & Glenda, and Ed, and Owen, and David Edelstein (yet another proud graduate of the *Phoenix*), are all up to cool, creative things. *Ich bin ein San Franciscan.* I have this quirky little career, making stories out of my life and performing them before brilliant, forgiving audiences. I work in a funky, sunny office filled with accomplished writers (including Po Bronson, whose idea this book was in the first place). And now— most unbelievably, perhaps—thanks to Mercury House (and their long-suffering transcribers, who are currently in the custody of the federal Intern Protection Program) I have my stories written down, Gutenberged for the masses (well, okay, maybe not the masses . . .).

And, to my immense surprise, this introduction has come out relatively quickly. Who knew (sorry, Tom Christensen and Kirsten Janene-Nelson at Mercury House!) that at thirty-seven I'd discover my writer's block to be cured, only to be replaced by . . . galley-proofer's block?!

I hope, dear reader, that you have enjoyed these stories as much as I've enjoyed telling them. But that, for your sake, you haven't sweat as much in the process.

—Josh Kornbluth
San Francisco
July 4, 1996